The Rockabilly Singer

MAXWELL PRICE

THE ROCKABILLY SINGER
An 18thWall Productions book published by
arrangement with Maxwell Price
verba mea in minibus
desiderium meum
Cover by Johannes Chazot
Jacket and Internal Design by M.H. Norris

ISBN-13: 978-1-946033-13-0

To Kris Hyatt,
Badder than Big Jim

One:
"Long distance information, give me Memphis Tennessee..."

It was fall, 1957. I was standing by the back door of a cocktail bar, taking a smoke break with the busboys. It shouldn't have been a rough gig that night. I had been hired to play background music for all the well-to-do diners, but the piano had been in a real mean mood and the whole affair had turned into a struggle against more destructive impulses. When you get down to it, a piano is a percussion instrument, full of cruel hammers colliding against tightly-wound steel. With the right touch, though, you can make all that violence come out as smooth and calming as the smoke from a freshly-lit cigarette. But just like the Lucky I was hitting, it was a temporary fix, paper-thin and fleeting. I watched the smoke curl up to the sky, where, as of the past week, we had something new to worry about floating overhead. Somewhere out between the smog and the stars was something called Sputnik; another little contraption of wire and metal to let us know that the future was finally here, and always watching. And we watched back, or at least cast nervous glances skywards. And at each other.

After the gig, I walked back to the cheap hotel that I called home. The man at the desk flagged me down, making my nicotine-stained heart thump a few extra beats. Had they finally decided to collect on the back rent I owed?

"Message for you, Cecil."

More debtors, most likely, or another supper club gig for pocket change. That's what I was expecting, anyway.

"Somebody called all the way from Memphis, Tennessee."

The desk clerk handed me a piece of paper where, in a crisp and orderly pen, there was an unfamiliar phone number, and a name I hadn't seen in seven years.

Big Jim was the last person I had expected to call with a paying gig. Usually it was the other way around, but for once I was the one that needed solid work. After the war, Jim and I had both served time playing in Carl Weber's Saddle Stompers. It was a pretty steady gig, at least until Carl wound up in prison for killing his third wife. The band split up, all of us scattering and heading to whichever city smelled the most like money. This meant that Big Jim ended up in Memphis, while I took a trip out to the west coast. Post-war California was honey and cream for hillbilly players, and I had found plenty of work playing studio sessions there in the early 50s. Did a lot of dances and radio shows for the homesick crackers that had moved west to work for the airlines and defense contractors. I even managed to sneak myself onto a few jazz gigs, but don't let that get around. Think of my reputation.

The more I thought about Jim's reputation, though, the more I figured I ought to place another phone call, to Junior White. He had played electric guitar in the Stompers, and according to Big Jim they had ended up with a back-up gig behind some young cat, traveling the south and making decent straw off playing sloppy and acting the fool.

"Oh, Cecil," Junior said, "it's hokum. Jim thumping the bass, trying to ride the damn thing like a horse. Wishing he was a teenager again."

Junior sounded embarrassed by it all, which was to be expected. Junior White was always a family man, and not much of a drinker. Whereas I think Big Jim's pitch included the exact phrase "more pussy than ten years of Saddle Stomping."

"I just stand there and pick," said Junior, "like any gig."

"Apparently this singer is something to see, from the way Jim talks."

"Well," sighed Junior, "the fella's a little strange, but the kids go nuts for him. Guys hooting and hollering, and the gals…I've never seen such. Nice while it lasts, I guess."

"And you're looking all the way out here for a piano player?"

"Well, we got a few recording sessions coming up, and plenty of gigs booked in-between 'em. Record company men want to use the usual Nashville guys, but Jim keeps bringing up your name. Truth is, it would be nice to have more grown folks to talk to."

"How can I say no? I guess this is my chance to see this rock-and-roll business up close."

Another sigh on the other end of the phone.

"Like I said, it's just another gig."

In a few days I made my last rounds in L.A., dispensing all the goodbyes and fare-thee-wells and kiss-my-asses I had in me. Then I hopped on a bus bound for Tennessee. On the way, I thought how it wasn't long ago that Big Jim, Junior, and I were playing jumped-up boogie riffs under hillbilly songs, and helping to sell more beers than we ever sold records. Now kids were buying up records like crazy, and a fair number of those bore more than a passing resemblance to the ones we had once cut. True, these new records featured singers that were thinner and younger than we had ever been—but suddenly the future didn't seem as bleak for a bunch of western bop has-beens. The west coast had lost its shine for me, anyway. All I had to look forward to was endless hustling, and the music I had been struggling to pay the bills with had gotten safe and bloodless. If I didn't watch out, I was going to end up old and bitter.

But enough about me.

You want to hear about the rockabilly singer.

To start with, here's the difference between the country singers we used to back up and the rockabilly singers that were becoming stars in 1957: country singers, back then, all projected a facade of squeaky-clean, tight-assed wholesomeness. This was to cover up the fact that the majority of them were pop-eyed crazy in one way or the other; crazy for booze or pills or pussy, or for things even more frowned-upon. This was all well and good in the honky-tonks, but in order to appeal to the new upwardly mobile consumers of post-war America, the old vices had to be subdued. Country was becoming a new kind of respectable pop music, with a fresh legion of lacquer-haired singers to match. But the old sins were hard to shake. And so the end would come, after the painkillers had eaten their insides, booze had ravaged their golden voices, or some married man had put a bullet in their guts. They would be found dead in the backseat of their new Cadillacs, or floating face-down in their guitar-shaped swimming pools, and an orgy of pious hand-wringing would commence. Sentimental tribute songs would be written. And the ones left would scrub their public image that much harder, shellacking their life stories until they gleamed, running the whole thing off a mix of false humility and maniacal self-promotion.

Country singers, in other words, were a bunch of twisted bastards that did their level best to appear dull and unthreatening.

Rockabilly singers, on the other hand, played up their eccentricities. They emphasized all manner of nervous tics, and they reveled in their rough edges. They sneered as much as they smiled. Elvis spat his gum out on the stage and told bad jokes in a marble-mouthed drawl. Gene Vincent stood swathed in black leather, his bad

9

leg splayed out at an odd angle. They piled their hair up, wore pink-and-green pastel suits, and they yelped and hollered like the microphone was giving off hot grease sparks. This was also a put-on. They too, did all of this to hide what they really were.

They were country singers.

At first glance, Bucky Bennett seemed to be cut from the same whiskey-and-semen-stained cloth as the others: just another hick with a twitchy voice and a battered, untuned guitar. His biggest hit so far was "Po-Dee Ro-Nee," an agreeable piece of gibberish that had gone over big in the Southeast. In it, Bucky's quavery voice hit the notes like a punch-drunken boxer, and sometimes only a glancing blow at that. But he had a way with his loopy phrases; some innate musical instinct kept things from falling apart. What he lacked in pitch, Bucky made up for in sheer novelty.

A strange-looking cat, too, at least in the publicity photo I had seen. Bucky wasn't a porcelain-cheeked cherub like Eddie or Elvis, but he wasn't a prematurely leathery old thing like Gene or Carl, either. The picture made him look like he had an old face under young skin— a little too much forehead and chin, a crooked grin and what they used to call "thyroid eyes." His eyebrows threatened to meet in the middle and have a rumble.

Big Jim and Junior were in the picture, too. Junior fingered a chord on a brand-new guitar and looked blandly amused, while Jim stood with one arm around his bass, head reared back and teeth bared in a pitiless grin. They were quite a trio, but the time had come to expand the ranks. A drummer was now mandatory, and it was decided that a barrelhouse piano-player would add drive and color to the proceedings.

That's when they decided to give me a call. Not to crow about it, but I'd like to think they had good reason to call me in, even though Memphis has to have more players per square foot than just about any place on Earth. The chemistry between me, Jim, and Junior had always been powerful, despite our differing personalities. They were also my friends, of course, but it makes you wonder. Do we play good together because we're friends, or are we all friends because we play good together?

As a sideman, I've always had a knack for making a shaky singer sound better; it's a thankless task, but often a profitable one. Doing it right means becoming invisible, creating a sound that floats in and flatters the singer the same way a big gob of Vaseline on the lens of a camera melts the years off a movie star. People nod their heads, they snap their fingers, and the spotlight never swings too far in the direction of the piano player.

I'd sat in front of a piano more than I'd done anything else in my life; certainly more than I ever studied or tried any honest work. More than I'd had sex, for sure. Eating came damn close, but I must qualify that by saying that if you've got a strong left hand and a good reach, you can get a fair amount done at most gigs. If I'm being

11

honest, though, I'd have to say that goes double for drinking.

Piano playing, drinking, and eating. Throw in a bathroom break, every now and then. Sleep had always been a distant fifth, even when I was a kid. Insomnia runs in the family, I suppose, but for a musician keeping odd hours it doesn't matter too much. I know it's supposed to be bad for you, but I could always get by on little sleep.

Of course, after everything that happened with Bucky, I had to learn to get by on even less.

One of the drawbacks to being a piano player is that you can't just hitch the instrument to your back like a guitar. The upside is, nobody expects you to; in those days, any honky-tonk worth a damn would have a jangling old upright in the corner. Of course, you never knew how reliable or in-tune they were, and I'd spent plenty of gigs dodging sour keys. In a nice recording studio, though, like the ones I'd been haunting out in California, nothing less than a baby grand would do.

This little sweatbox of a studio that Big Jim had lured me to had a beat-up old spinet that got blurry in the higher octaves. Still, I'd played much worse in my day, and I figured I'd get warmed up a little before the other fellas showed. I had arrived in Memphis earlier that afternoon, having spent most of the bus ride staring out the window and trying not to second-guess myself. Aside from those few phone calls, I hadn't heard from Jim or Junior since the Saddle Stompers disbanded. Not that we'd had any particular kind of falling out. I had just gotten the feeling that if I kept running with Jim I'd be dead before I hit thirty. Now that we had both made it at least that far, maybe things would be a touch more mellow.

I ran through a few stride pieces, then I tried out a few chords that I'd been hearing at some of the jazz dates out west. I had just hung a particularly foggy cluster of notes over the room when I heard somebody bellow my name, and say—

"Oh hell, you shoulda dumped all that egg-headed shit in the Pacific ocean before you even got packed. You play any of that stuff and them kids will scatter like quail!"

It was Big Jim. A few pounds heavier, his skin crinkling a little more around his eyes, but still the same stone-ignorant son-of-bitch. God, I loved him like a brother.

"Oh, I know, Jimbo. I took a listen to that record you all put out. You're looking for that hillbilly gospel shit, aren't you?" I demonstrated with a few lard-greased phrases that tore a smile across Jim's face.

"Now you're talking! It don't make the cut unless it can pass the 'stupid test.'"

"If it sounds good twice..."

"Play it again!"

We both roared, and Big Jim gave me a swat on the back that felt like it popped a few things out of whack. Next to enter the studio was Junior White, guitar case and dour expression in hand, though he relaxed a bit when me and Jim started cutting up. The drummer snuck in behind him; made us all jump, in fact, when he started practicing his rudiments on the beat-up studio kit. I looked over and saw a baby sitting behind an oversized bass drum. He was introduced as Dickie, and I suppose he was there to balance out the three old farts in the band, because he had to have been plucked from some high school marching band. He had a nervous smile and a jumpy leg. Still, during the two or three weeks he had been in the band the kid had learned how to follow Big Jim's bass thumping pretty good, and he had learned how to follow Jim's drinking and pill-popping even better than that.

Instruments were tuned; recording levels were set. A bottle of whiskey appeared and wandered around the room, and soon we were warmed-up and ready to go. At about twenty after, Bucky showed up, along with a little bald man from the record company. Even in the heat, the record company man had his sleeves buttoned-up, and he wore a silk tie pulled so tight that you would have thought it was the only thing keeping his head attached. Bucky was in blue jeans and a peppermint-striped shirt that was unbuttoned halfway down his scrawny chest. He made his way around the room, joking with the other guys, taking swigs of whiskey, and chomping on fried peanuts that he had brought in a greasy paper bag.

Seeing him in person for the first time, I was surprised. He was taller than I had thought, though he was always tilting his head to the side, and the way his shoulders leaned over indicated a crooked back. Maybe it was from toting

14

around one of those new electric guitars, but it seemed more likely it was the result of manual labor, started much too young, or maybe a just nasty spill from a motorcycle. His records presented him as someone coming unhinged, but in truth he had an easygoing charm and an animated physical presence. Bucky could be like that, when he wanted to. He made an introduction, bummed a cigarette, and like that I was accepted into the band.

The man from the record company drank no whiskey, and said not a word to anyone in the band. He joined the engineer in the control room, and the first time we heard him speak, it was broadcast over the loudspeaker in the corner.

"Alright, Buck, we're got the demo here for your next single, and we're ready to play it. Would you like to come in here to listen?"

Bucky pulled up one of the folding chairs and sat, propping his feet up on the bass drum and popping another peanut in his mouth.

"Aw hell, I'll sit out here with the troops. Go on, let 'er rip."

The record man's sigh was not broadcast over the loudspeaker. He motioned to the engineer, who started up a turntable and fiddled with the mixing board until the sound of a cheaply-pressed acetate crackled out of the loudspeaker.

The voice of the man on the demo bore a passing resemblance to man from the record company's; it's likely they were related. He sang in a weedy tenor, and it was obvious to all of us

that his song was a pale imitation of the first
single that Bucky had cut. It was also obvious
that there would be no discussing this with the
man from the record company.

Presently the man on the acetate began to
yodel.

Every musician in the room instinctively
threw his gaze to the floor, fighting the urge to
laugh. I couldn't see in the control room that
well, but it was possible that even the engineer
was clutching his pearls and wincing in pain.
The record ended and Bucky turned to face the
band.

"Well boys, looks like it's time to go to
work."

A half-hour later we had torn that song a fresh
one, and landed Bucky Bennett his first top
twenty hit. We threw the yodeling out and put a
guitar break in its place. It still gets played on
the radio occasionally, and I've lost track of how
many people have asked me about it. What kind
of guitar did y'all use, what kind of amp, and
who is that hollering in the background? (Just
for the record, Big Jim does the first one, then
Dickie does the high-pitched one after the piano
solo). As far as my own contributions, I
hammered the chords into the ground, and then
slid up and down the keys like I was playing
with an oven mitt. Kids ate it up with a spoon.

The other song we cut that day, once everybody
settled in, was strange even by the standards of
rockabilly. It was in a minor key, for one thing,

but still taken at that same nervous, itchy tempo. Bucky hummed a little three-note riff to Junior, who tried to dress it up the best he could, though he still sat and played with the expression of a man destined for the dentist's chair. That didn't matter to Dickie, who took the rhythm of the little riff and elaborated on it with splashing cymbals and crisp rimshots. Bucky had instructed the beleaguered engineer to really crank the echo, and as it made ghosts of the last few notes of the guitar solo, he stepped up to the mic and sang:

> *Come away, O honey child!*
> *To the waters, and the wild*
> *With your daddy, hand in hand,*
> *For the world's more fulla weeping than*
> *   you understand*
> *Yeah, more fulla weeping than you*
> *   understand*

When Bucky was through with the verse he cut me a bug-eyed glance, indicating that I was to take over where he left off. I took a solo, not pounding or sliding this time, but making the keys really ring, even throwing in a few jazz licks that might get me slapped down. To hell with it, I thought. I ended with a shivery little series of arpeggios, just repetitive enough to pass the "stupid test," and the high-pitched cackle from over by the microphone told me that I was doing fine.

And that was that. A few hours gone by, a

17

handful of sides cut, and we were done. Not bad for an afternoon's work.

As the other boys were packing up, I happened to step out into the hallway just in time to catch Bucky and the little man from the record company going at it.

"Listen here Mr. Kirby, they told me I could have the flip-side of the third single, and that's what I want!"

"Son, you just don't get it. They mean to say that you can pick which song ends up on the b-side. Pick—as in, choose from the songs that we already own the publishing rights to. I keep trying to tell you, you don't have to write your own material, we have people for that."

"But that song means something to me. I've been hearing it in my head since I was just a baby! My mama must have sung it to me or something..."

"Even more reason to pass," said the record company man, "on account of your mama doesn't have a publishing deal!"

At that, Bucky grabbed Mr. Kirby by his collar and slammed him against the wall.

"You just listen, goddammit! I've had that song in my head so long it's fit to bust, and your boss told me that I could pick the b-side! Well, I'm picking THAT SONG, you understand?"

Suddenly Bucky was turning red, the veins in his neck popping out like high-tension wires. The noise brought the others out into the hall, and they pulled Bucky off of Mr. Kirby. The record company man was shaking like a leaf, and having lost some wind, he just barely managed to get his reply out.

"Alright! God-almighty! We'll just put your name on it, and we'll work out the publishing details, but you better hope to God that it doesn't hold the record up! Wait too long to get the records out, and we'll all be stranded at the goddamn station, watching some other fool kid make his run up the charts!"

As Mr. Kirby slunk off, cursing and choking, Big Jim loosened his grip on Bucky's rail-thin arm. He turned to us sheepishly, his voice hushed and fragile.

"Sorry, fellas. I-I just had that song in my head for so long. You know how is it when you get something stuck in your head like that?"

"You just gotta get it out."

Two:
"We're going to rip it up..."

The next night we went back to the studio to start rehearsing for the gigs that Bucky's handlers had booked. Far from the prying ears of the company men, we finished off the whiskey, and by the time rehearsal was over we ended up with a pretty good set. There were the handful of singles that Bucky was obliged to do live, and the strange, wild b-side we had tossed off the other day. We did several other recent rock-and-roll hits: "Rip it Up," "Blue Suede Shoes," and "Maybellene." We mixed in some tunes that we used to do in the Saddle-Stomper days, like "Corrine, Corrina" and "Blues Stay Away From Me." To that we added rhythm-and-blues songs by Wynonie Harris, Louis Jordan, Lloyd Price, and Charles Brown. Bucky even warbled his way through a spooky version of Merle Travis' "Dark as a Dungeon." Not bad for a couple of green kids and a trio of over-the-hill western players. We got the changes down, the beat got a little bolder, and Junior almost cracked a smile. Bucky's singing started to relax, though it always kept a shiver in it.

Eventually Junior and Jim drifted off; Junior went home to his wife and Jim left to look for more whiskey. Dickie had similarly vanished, and Bucky sat at the piano with me trading gospel songs.

"Cecil, you've got a hell of a touch," he said, as the last notes of "Leaning on the Everlasting Arms" faded like evening mist.

"Aw shit," I said, slurring, "I do my best. You want to hear something, you ought to listen to the old stride players."

"Is that right?"

"Oh yeah. I grew up on that stuff. I was raised by my Aunt Nora; she played piano in church every Sunday, but she also had every record Fats Waller ever made."

"Well, that's something, Mr. Cecil," said Bucky. "Maybe you can show me something on the piano someday..."

"Maybe," I said. "I never gave any lessons before." Honestly, though, he was already a pretty decent player, in a church-y, backwoods style. I remember thinking at the time that the guy's fingers were even longer than mine; they made his hands look like frail spiders stalking the keys.

Bucky paused for a second. "Raised by an Aunt, huh?"

"Yep," I said. "Daddy was a son-a-bitch, ran off, never met him. Mama couldn't afford me, so Nora took me in."

"You know, Mr. Cecil, I never knew my Daddy either. It's a hell of a thing."

I started off another tune, something a little

brighter, before things got too godawful depressing.

"Oh, I don't know," I said, "Nora done the best she could, which was probably better than most. I didn't end up working for a living, so it's quite all right."

Bucky cracked up at that one.

"Although if you keep calling me 'Mr. Cecil,' I'm afraid you might give me a complex."

Our conversation was cut short by the sound of Dickie's snoring. We looked behind the guitar amplifiers and found him curled up on the floor, clutching the empty whiskey bottle like a kid with a teddy bear.

The first gig was that Friday, at a big auditorium that was miles away from the cramped honky-tonks that I had played in my youth. On the bill were two or three straight country singers, a gospel quartet, and a hayseed comedian, with Bucky Bennett and the Blue-tone Bops dropped down in the middle like a contingent of visiting Martians. An audience of nervous young things milled around between sets, and the security was provided by the kind of thick-necked sheriff's deputy-types I usually tried to avoid. We had all of twenty minutes to knock the crowd on their ass before making way for the next act.

Backstage, Junior ran scales, Dickie drummed on the back of a chair. Big Jim stood with his arms folded, popping gum, one leg on his battered old upright bass, which lay sideways on the cold concrete floor. Bucky leaned against

23

the wall and tried not to look anxious.

Out on the stage a red-headed firecracker of a singer was going off, and her name was Miss Alta Moore. Today people remember Alta for syrupy ballads, but back when she was doing the package shows she sang honky-tonk and rockabilly. Problem was, she was just too damn good at it. She'd twist her red, lip-sticked mouth around a couple of blue notes and guys would get all sorts of unwholesome ideas. Back then America preferred its kittens to purr or cry, but Alta yowled and spit when she sang rock-n-roll.

Applause signaled the end of Alta's set, and as her band trotted off the stage she stayed for a bit of banter with the MC, a crazy fella by the name of Dewey who talked like he had taken a fistful of Dexedrine at the start of the show and was still chewing 'em. They a had a routine worked up about red hair (they both had it, though Dewey's was already moving back) and Alta's young age, and she was a good sport for the dirty old goat. Then Dewey started our introduction.

Ladies and gentleman, hepcats and kitties, you all are going to love this next boy, he's the long gone geek with the big bad beat, he's got stars in his eyes and gold in his teeth and alligator shoes a-bopping beneath, he drives the wimmin wild with his hair in a pile about three feet from heaven, he's seven-come-eleven—

I think Dewey would have gone on all night if Bucky hadn't suddenly appeared on stage, grabbed the microphone like he was about to throttle it, and sang the longest, loudest, and wildest "wellllllll" any of those kids had ever heard. When we hit the downbeat they all screamed like their lungs were about to burst, and Bucky's body jerked like he was plugged into a light socket. Dewey stood aside and howled with laughter that was lost in the eruption of sound. He jumped and laughed and slapped his hand on his knee; a cartoon hillbilly lost in reverie. It wasn't so much that somebody had the stones to interrupt Dewey—the kids all loved Dewey, too—it was just the sheer joy of a genuine, unscripted rock-and-roll moment. That was rare even back then, and if it fulfilled just a thimble-full of what the music promised, that was enough. It gave you a feeling like things were changing. Life was going to be different. Things were getting better.

That was when I figured out where Bucky's real talents lie. He was weird-looking, couldn't play much guitar, and his singing wasn't going to make Sinatra fall out of his chair. But he could take an audience in the palm of his hand and hold them there all night. I thought then that it was precisely because he seemed so homely, his talent so raw, that you could feel the tension of somebody working hard, holding his own against the more polished singers. Even now, I can't really do it justice—he would grip the microphone stand so hard his knuckles were white, slick with sweat and singing like a man in the throes of religious ecstasy. He played those kids better than I ever played any instrument, and yet with his modest looks and halting Sunday-school manners, he didn't even seem to

25

realize it.

After the show we all sat and basked in the afterglow, passing more whiskey around and mingling with musicians, managers, and other hangers-on. Dewey and the other radio men held court, trying to find out who had the best dirty jokes. Even the record company man gave a cautious smile, like he had heard the keening cry of cash registers off in the distance.

Alta was there, too. She was only a few years older than Dickie. But she was laughing, drinking, and smoking right along with all of the others. She was beginning to get away from the days when her daddy would lead her from gig to gig, scowling at anybody that tried to say more than two words to her. Most of the guys there wouldn't have tried to pick her up anyway. There were plenty of well-gartered girls around who didn't have to worry about upsetting any overprotective showbiz daddies. So it was "Miss Moore" to most of the guys in the band.

Didn't stop Bucky, though. He was riding a buzz that was half Johnnie Walker and half adrenaline-pumping applause, a potent mix. He still was playing the shy bumpkin, but something had come over him; he didn't seem quite as ungainly as before. His posture suggested someone more sturdy than the stoop-shouldered punk I'd met the previous day.

But then, why not? They were both young, and both had sold a few records with their names on them. They were both ready to be stars. Bucky beamed. Alta glowed like a summer

26

sunset.

"Hey Alta," said Bucky, gesturing towards me, "have you met my new piano player? This is Cecil Jones. Whatever you do, don't call him Mr. Cecil, you'll never hear the end of it."

"Cecil Jones," said Alta, "there's an interesting name."

"He's an interesting guy, is Cecil," said Bucky, "and playing with him makes me feel like I'm punching way above my weight. We had to pull Cecil all the way from Los Angeles for this gig."

Bucky put his hand on Alta's shoulder. They both smiled. I thought, is he showing her off to me or me to her? Made me feel a little embarrassed.

Just then, Big Jim came walking up with Coca-Colas for him and Dickie. A nice fatherly gesture, but if you looked closely you could see a pair of Benzedrine strips (torn out of asthma inhalers) floating in the bottles. There were pills around, too, if anybody wanted to indulge. You could have something to take the edge off, or you could sharpen that edge like a razor. The musical sounds of laughter carried on until dawn.

When you start playing with somebody, there comes a point when you have to decide whether or not you're going to be giving it your all, or just biding your time until the real thing comes along. It sounds like a cold thing, I know. People—people who don't play—hear it and they figure you're just a hack. But music is a

27

funny, fickle thing. Once you turn pro, you learn how to play solid without having to throw yourself on the trench wire every time. Give too much to any bandleader and you'll end up as heartbroken as anyone left standing at the altar. Chase those sounds in your head too far, and there too, lies a world of hurt and embitterment. Better to be a weekend romantic, rationing it out in manageable doses, and saving yourself for the great times. The truly transcendent times.

I remember when I started to think that playing with Bucky could be more than just a pleasant lost weekend for an aging rhythm player like myself. We were sitting in a diner somewhere after one of the early Memphis shows, giving the gig and everybody at it the usual post-mortem. I was drinking cup after cup of coffee and Buck was snuffing cigarette butts in a plate that was empty, save for a generous puddle of maple syrup.

"You're the brains," he said, stretching the band over another metaphor. It was a game he liked to play. Sometimes the band was a Cadillac or a train. Tonight the band was a mule.

"I'd be flattered, if we weren't talking mule brains."

"Smarter than a horse."

"I suppose. So about the rest of the boys?"

"Junior is the hooves—old and hard, but he gets us where we need to go. Dickie and Jim are the back muscles, because we've got them doing all the hard work."

"That must make you the back-end."

"No, I've got a better one," said Bucky,

stifling a laugh. "I'll be the mule's cods. That way I can hang around and not do shit."

We both howled. Unfortunately, the sounds of tear-soaked laughter brought the attention of some good ol' boys from a few tables over. They came and stood by us, sunburned arms crossed over their chests. Three of them, all looking like they chewed on sheet metal for fun. Not an autograph seeker among them.

"Something seem funny to you boys?" The one who spoke first had a voice like a grinding gearbox, the kind that would never sing songs for young girls to scream over.

"We were just talking about mule cods," said Bucky, giving me a wink. I couldn't help it, I started laughing again.

Rusty Gearbox gave me a look that let me know that he didn't like me at all, even if he couldn't put his finger on why yet. His buddy decided to give it a shot.

"It's like they're laughing at us," he said, in a similarly unlovely voice. His sounded a little more like a frog with smoker's cough.

"Well, that's just rude as hell," said Gearbox, "bunch of no-good degenerates laughing at hard-working Christians like ourselves."

"Yeah," added Froggy Throat, "not everybody here has stayed up all night playing blue-gum music and chasing poon. Some of us are just getting off third shift."

The third guy didn't say anything at all, he just snorted as if he were gathering up a prize-winning loogie under his tongue.

"C'mon, fellas," said Bucky, grinding his last

29

cigarette into his plate. "We don't want any trouble. It's been a long night for everybody. We didn't mean any harm, did we, Cecil?"

I was trying to think of something diplomatic, but just then that prize-winning loogie did a swan dive into my coffee. Don't Talk Much broke into a scummy grin.

In a disgusted reflex, I swatted the cup away, which just happened to send coffee flying everywhere. Rusty and Froggy took direct hits, shielding Don't Talk Much from most of the blast.

Next thing I knew, Rusty had his hands all around the collar of my brand-new pearl-buttoned shirt, ready to hoist me to my feet and deliver unto me a ferocious ass whipping. From the look in his eye, he seemed to have finally figured out why he didn't like me so much.

"You piece of trash," he said, "you no good, worthless—"

He had a few more choice words about me, but Bucky cut him off.

"Let's step outside," said Bucky, "how about it?" He had placed his hand over Rusty's, and it no longer looked frail and spidery to me. Feeling the weight of it as it lifted the other man's grip away from my collar, it seemed improbably large, lined with ice-blue veins and sporting knuckles like pine knots.

Everyone in the diner was staring now. Only a few hours earlier, we were playing in front of scores of adoring teenagers; now I could feel the hard eyes of what could have been their parents and uncles, waiting for these guys to take us both down a notch.

Now, if Big Jim had been there, it would have already been over. Jim could have simply broken the guy's finger while he sipped on a whiskey-stiffened coffee and asked the waitress for another round of french fries. Or more likely, he would have simply told a joke so filthy that even our humorless new companions would have let out a titter, and we all would have greeted the coming dawn by getting sloppy drunk together.

Back when we played to rough crowds every night, I came to rely on Big Jim to keep anybody from breaking my shins or beating me senseless. And while he kept us out of plenty of jams, I sometimes got to resent the way he didn't have to fight guys like this if he didn't want to. If it wasn't for the likes of me, there probably wouldn't have been as many problems. And I came to wonder if he didn't resent me back, just a little bit. With Bucky, though, it was different.

"We don't want any trouble," he said, "and you don't want any trouble either."

"And yet, here we are," said Rusty.

"If it's come to that," said Bucky, "let's step outside."

Rusty reached for my collar again, but Bucky put his hand out again.

"No sir, my piano player needs his hands." Laughter all around. "I tell you what," he continued, "you three whip me and you can come back for him."

Satisfied with the arrangement, the trio of Rusty, Froggy, and Don't Talk Much filed out the door behind Bucky. A crowd started to press against the front windows, but I just sat at the table, ashamed and terrified. Maybe I had stayed in Los Angeles too long to come back to the South.

As it was, the crowd didn't have much of an idea of what was going on, either, on account of the first thing Bucky did was walk behind the diner, out of sight.

"That boy's crazy..."

"...someone ought to call the police..."

"...more like an ambulance..."

"...going to grease the axle on that boy's car..."

"...well they play that awful jungle music..."

"...look!"

Here came Froggy and Don't Talk Much, running like the devil himself was after them. They didn't even stop by to pay their bill. Rusty limped after them, blood flowing from his nose. After about a minute Bucky came back inside, rolling up his sleeves, a freshly-lit cigarette between his lips. He came back inside the diner just long enough to leave a wad of bills at our table, then we both hustled our way out into the night. He never spoke a word about it after that. Never made me feel like I owed him. But after that, I would have followed the guy to the mouth of hell.

Of course, Bobby Dwayne had a different impression of Bucky. From the first package tour he was giving us all the hairiest eyeball he could muster, which given the rug he used to wear, might have been the only hirsute part left on his noggin.

Bobby Dwayne was another stone country singer who had found himself ass-over-teakettle in the brave new world of rock-and-roll. Mama and Jesus suddenly had to make room for pink Cadillacs and red blue jeans. Facing musical oblivion, Bobby held his nose and sang a few rockabilly sides through clenched teeth, then cursed his luck when one of them charted. He found himself out on the road with the likes of Bucky and Alta, playing to rooms full of pimply brats, and he wasn't shy about letting everybody know how pissed off he was about the whole thing. A few drinks would be all it would take, and he'd be stomping around backstage and ranting about how this country was going to fall to the communists on account of the white man lowering himself to the level of the coons and the Catholics.

Bucky or Big Jim would always say *gosh Bobby, tell us how you really feel*, and then he would get real mad. Rusty and Froggy were probably his biggest fans.

You can read all about this in *Untold Stories of Rock and Roll* and a couple other disreputable tomes, though they tend to skip over it in Bobby Dwayne's biographies. At least, that's one version. Years later, after everything that happened, I've got a few theories of my own.

The story I heard goes like this: Bobby shot his mouth off one time too many, and said something that pissed Bucky off but good. Maybe something about his music, or maybe

how he didn't like a greased-up punk making off
with a nice country gal like Alta. Nobody knows
what Bobby said, but it must have been the kind
of thing that makes a man stew for a couple
days. The kind of thing that won't let go.
Because one night Bucky got Bobby drunk and
took him to a run-down motel, and got back at
him so he'd never forget. When they found
Bobby two days later, he was dehydrated and
half insane, with the singed remains of his
hairpiece still fastened tightly across his
blistered noggin. He also had to have two of the
toes on his right foot amputated.

In most accounts, the story is that Bucky
pulled a gun on Bobby, and made him dance
until his feet bled. Kept him awake for two days,
forcing him to do all those other things to
himself. Sat and drank whiskey, laughing, while
Bobby pleaded and begged for his life.

It's a story that makes Bucky look like a
psycho, crazier than even Jerry Lee himself. But
no charges were ever pressed against Bucky—at
least, not that we ever knew. It would have been
quite a feat, too, because for those two days that
Bucky was supposed to be happily torturing
Bobby Dwayne, he was out playing one-nighters
with us. It would have been impossible for him
to have done any of that. But Bobby, when he
got drunk enough to talk about it, still blamed
Bucky for everything. And who wanted to let a
little fact-checking get in the way of a good tale
of rock-and-roll Babylon?

So what's the truth? I don't think Bucky
would have held a gun on Bobby Dwayne for

two days straight. I don't think he needed a gun. I think maybe all it would have taken was for him to snap his fingers, or wave his hand, or maybe sing something stranger and more secret than anything he ever did with us. And then Bobby would have been compelled to do those terrible things to himself; he wouldn't have been able to help it, just like the kids at the shows we played seemed to go into fits and spasms when Bucky hit the stage. Hell, maybe Bucky did something to Bobby and didn't even know it; nobody would ever accuse a rockabilly singer of being the most self-aware person in the world. He might have thought he just told Bobby off, walked out of that motel room, and left before all the bad craziness unfolded.

Like I say, I don't think Bucky knew the power he had, or where it came from. That was what caused his downfall, in the end. But a lot of good that did for poor Bobby, whose sentimental ditties came roaring back to the charts, but who never did sleep through the night again. Thirty years and a couple million records later, you'd think the edge might've come off, but I have it on good authority that even today, the merest mention of Bucky Bennett is enough to send Bobby Dwayne into fits of rage and feral panic. If things went the way I think they did, those two days must have been a nightmare come to life for Bobby, a confirmation of every nasty thing he ever suspected about this ugly new music and the world it infected. Poor Bobby Dwayne, who never even liked that rock-and-roll shit in the first place.

The world turned. All through late '57 and into '58, the great commie rock-and-roll menace continued to stick its finger in the collective ear of all the Bobby Dwaynes of middle America. Not content with merely poisoning the airwaves, rockers also polluted the silver screen with their greased-up presence. "Great Balls of Fire" came out, and Chuck Berry, looking diabolically dapper with his thin mustache and slicked-back hair, sang expertly-crafted ditties about "School Days" and "Sweet Little Sixteen." Link Wray released an instrumental so crude and malevolent-sounding it was banned on the radio. Little Susie woke up and mom and dad hoped to God she wasn't pregnant.

We even made an album. *The Blue-Tones Bop the Rock* was recorded over two days in that sweat-box of a studio, its contents a dog's dinner of blues covers, rockabilly riffs, and shlock lyrics courtesy of Mr. Kirby's yodeling half-brother. The cover features the band hunched in the corner while Bucky's pale, otherworldly mug takes up most of the space. His bug-eyes are closed for once, and his expression hovers somewhere between ecstasy and pain as he opens his mouth to sing.

That record is a collector's item today, because it didn't sell for shit the first time around. Our album sank where our singles flew, mostly due to circumstances beyond our control. The record company had distribution problems, and it struggled to get the record to the towns we were playing. By the time you could pick up

Bop the Rock in the stores, we were miles away, just a distant ringing in the ears of the kids who had seen and then forgotten us in favor of some newer hit. Mr. Kirby turned red in the face, and intimated of unseen conspiracies coming together to screw us over in the bad old world of show business. In the end it didn't matter much to us—those really were great times, and even a grasping chance at a piece of greatness was enough to set your world aglow.

We played to mixed audiences, not the first I'd ever seen, but certainly the biggest and the youngest. Sure, they had the white kids up in the balcony and the black kids down on the floor, but that just seemed to drive home how absurd it all was; you could see how bad the white kids wanted to be on the floor, too, where it was easier to dance. But mostly they screamed like banshees, all of them, just wanting to hear some music that kicked and howled and bit.

Buck, in particular, seemed to soak up the adulation like a sponge. And the strangest thing started to happen—Bucky started to change. His slouch disappeared. He put on weight; not puppy fat from too many greasy diner meals, but real lean muscle. Even his hair stood up straighter. Now, most of this can be explained by the fact that we were all riding higher in the saddle than we had been a few months ago. After all, a young man gets a little taste of success, both professional and personal, and it's bound to have an effect. Confidence can do wonders, plus he had Alta to help him pick out his slick new suits.

But confidence can't change the color of

37

your eyes: his had turned from grey to blue, so gradually that you had a hard time believing it was just a pair of contact lenses he had popped in one day. And confidence can't change the shape of your face: Buck was suddenly sporting a cleft chin that would make a matinee idol jealous. Again, it was hard to say—had it appeared overnight, or we were all just now noticing it? Now, the world was starting to make note of Bucky, and if he had snuck off to a plastic surgeon you'd think somebody would have wrote it up in the gossip rags. Hell, you'd think one of us would've at least noticed Bucky wearing a bandage for a few days.

There was something there that seemed odd, if you thought about it for a while. But nobody was in danger of doing much of that. This is America. A man can buy himself a brand new face, and much else besides, if he's got enough cash sitting around. I guess we didn't bother ourselves about any more about it than Carl Perkins' band did when he showed up one day with capped teeth and a toupee so tall it could've gone into business for itself.

As for myself, I was busy with my own miraculous transformation. Every time the crowds screamed and cried and the gals nearly wet themselves, I felt like all that noise was running through me like a river, and coming out my fingertips. I could have felt like a cynical old crank, slumming with a rock-and-roll band, but I was having fun again. I played like a much younger man.

It lasted about eight months, all told, and

Three:
"Little footprints in the snow..."

then it all went to shit.

Jim folded his paper over, and I could see a headline on the back pages:

LITTLE GREEN MEN?
RESIDENTS REPORT STRANGE LIGHTS IN
APPALACHIA

He caught me staring. We were seated across from each other, trying to choke down enough black coffee and overcooked diner food to make through the rest of the day.

"Don't you go sayin' it ain't possible. You don't know doodle squat."

"I hadn't said a word, Jim."

"Well, you kinda got that look in your eye. I know that look."

"You ought to."

"I know what you're thinking," he said, tapping his forehead, "you thinking I should learn to listen to that look of yours."

"Well," I said, "something like that. You've seen it enough."

"The last time I saw that look," he said,

scanning his paper again, "it was at that little drive-in chapel in Vegas."

"Yes, Jim."

"And you were trying, with that look of yours, to insinuate that I shouldn't have married that gal with the pout and the legs up to her neck."

"Jim, you know that gal took off a week later. Also, she took all your money, threw your clothes in a dumpster, and sold your bass to the pawn shop."

"No, it was the one in Tulsa that pawned the thing. The one in Vegas stole it and chucked it into Lake Mead, or least, that's what people told me when I went sniffin' for her."

Jim leaned back in his chair. We had both folded our arms together, without quite having realized it.

"Well," I said, "what do you make of that, Jim?"

"Ha," he said, slapping his knee, "it shows you still don't know squat!"

I must have rolled my eyes.

"Now, listen, Cecil," he said, "I miss that bass. A fine instrument. And I miss the gal, too. She was the only thing had more curves than that bass."

All of the sudden, Jim got a look of his own. His brow furrowed and I could very nearly see a little mist around the corners of his eyes.

"And sure, she ran off and left me naked, broke, and bass-less. Some gals just ain't the marrying kind. But you know what? That weekend in Vegas, she showed me more tricks than a magic show. And when I'm an old man, tucked away in a veteran's hospital somewheres, dick all dried up, brain turned to mush—I will still have that memory."

He unfolded his arms from his chest and then crossed them the other way, grabbing himself by the shoulders and rocking back and forth, grinning.

"I'll take that memory, and I'll just wrap myself up in it, like a blanket."

"Uh-huh," I said, "and not the memory of waking up hung over, head pounding, heart broken, and her making for another state with all your gig money."

"Well, that's where you and me differ. Time rolls on, the bad things get smaller and smaller in the rear view. That's my philosophy. Whereas you—"

He shook his rolled-up newspaper at me.

"You dwell on that stuff. Let it get to you. Throw yourself an old pity-party. And as a consequence, that bad stuff sorta takes over the landscape. Rises up, like a big damned mountain."

"And this has what to do with those little green men?"

"Now that is something else you just don't know about. I'm telling you, there's more to it than you think. Now, you were just in the merchant marines during the war. You didn't get to hang around the flyboys, like I did on my way into Berlin. Those guys had some stories."

Jim put his paper down.

"Those boys were zipping around trying to

fight the Luftwaffe. They didn't have much idle time to let their minds wander. Now, you get those boys drunk and they start to bragging. Drink a little more and they start confessing— we all did plenty of things that we'd rather not had to do. Drink a little more and, believe it or not, those flyboys would start telling you the damnedest things. Like how they got to chasing after little lights that moved like the devil and disappeared when you got too close."

"And when we rolled in to the German cities, got ahold of their pilots, and started asking them questions? More of the same! Silver disks darting over German airspace! Flashing orbs hovering over France and Belgium! It's just too many individual stories not to add to something!"

"Air's awful thin up there, Jim."

"Oh, come on! These are genuine flying aces we're talking about!"

"What about all the other stories? Like, all of the guys that saw little critters crawling around on their planes, fouling up the works?"

"That's not the same—I mean, there aren't nearly as many stories floating around—"

"But there's your little green men, right? What am I missing here?"

"Those are just superstitions. That's for people that can't live with the modern times."

"So what are the saucers?"

"They're the future, bearing down on us. I figure the new atom bombs and such are causing some kind of upset in the galaxy. It's like if ants or mice or something were suddenly building little tanks and rolling around. I mean, you'd want to keep an eye on that, look out for any new developments."

"Uh-huh."

"Me personally? I like this new modern world well enough. I'm partial to this rock-and-roll stuff, anyways, though the two of us have been playing something like it for half our lives."

Just then, a young woman walked by in a flower print dress. She too, was shaped like the bass fiddle, or perhaps a big bartlett pear in heels. Jim gestured at me with his paper, re-folded now to put the saucer article front and center.

"Look over it, brother," he said, "and see if it don't make a little more sense."

Most of us that play, we carry around somebody else inside of us, and that's the Guy on Stage. He's every bit the star, but usually a prick. It feels good to be the Guy on Stage, though, and sometimes you want that guy to step offstage, so you can impress a gal or throw back a few more drinks or maybe just walk taller for a little while. I think Big Jim must have got a big hurt laid on him somewhere, or else he got fed up with the particulars of day-to-day life and he decided hell, I'm just going to be that Guy on Stage all the damn time. Everything bad or good about Jim was all sewed up in that, in the person he made up for himself.

First off, any thought given to quitting music or getting a solid job was dismissed out of hand, regardless of years of frustration and setbacks. The Guy on Stage simply would not permit it. Nor was any kind of physical or mental pain ever an issue. I had seen Big Jim play hung-over, sick, hungry, and once after chewing a button of peyote. That was an interesting gig. Several times I saw him play until he had worn all the skin off of his thumb and his fingertips; he would just laugh, pour whiskey over the wounds and then fill them up with crazy glue.

He also did one string of gigs where he managed, as if by some twisted miracle, to get in a fight with a different mean-ass drunk every night, each one not only bigger than Jim himself, but also bigger and meaner than the previous evening's opponent. By the end of the week his hands looked like a couple of glazed hams someone had decided to drag across a gravel parking lot. And still Big Jim thumped away at the bass, harder and louder than ever, his mitts wrapped in bits of old washcloth that were held in place with dried blood. It wasn't until months later he told me they had sent him a telegram earlier that week, letting him know his daddy had died.

That kind of relentless dedication to the art is admirable, but unfortunately for Jim, he decided that his noble sacrifice absolved him of any other responsibilities that might crop up. Those couple of hours a night when you were playing beside him, he was the most disciplined, reliable guy on the planet—for Jim would just as soon cut an inch off his pecker than drop a beat. Drummers may drag and singers may go off-key, and hell, the bar could pretty much burn to the ground, but Big Jim would thump through it all, steady as a watch. Disciplined—but off the stage, not so much. He was moody and mercurial; he stayed up for days at a time, then slept right up until show time. Money burned holes in his pockets; whiskey and pills often threatened to burn through his insides. He tempted fate as a full-time occupation.

We had been on the road all through the fall and winter, hopping from show to show, tour to tour. We started playing with bigger names, real rock-and-roll names; we no longer had to suffer through opening for has-been country singers and hayseed comedians. We traveled beyond the south, out of the Bible Belt and into cities where vice didn't always come served with a deep-fried helping of guilt. Consequently, we all began to indulge a little more, which gave the music a reckless charge. But that's how it always is: get on the road long enough, work up some steam, and it's the Mongols and the Vikings all over again.

A show in St. Louis found us playing in the middle of a blizzard that left the locals unfazed but had my poor Georgia-raised ass frozen solid. Fortunately, we were holed up in our motel rooms with enough whiskey to last us through two or three winters, if necessary. Bucky sat on his bed, next to Alta, cradling a fine and pricey new guitar in his arms. We were passing songs back and forth again, but not gospel songs; this time it was strictly drinking songs. Besides the usual blues and hillbilly melodies, Bucky turned out versions of "The Wild Rover" and "The Moonshiner." The more we drank, the better he sang, and the more he sang, the smoother and more powerful the liquor seemed to become. It took on a deeper potency, one that softened the edges of the world without turning them to mush.

"Those old songs," said Alta. She brushed back a few stray curls. "I heard that Don and Phil Everly are in Nashville right now recording an album of songs like that."

"We could've beat them to it," I said. "We'd call it *Songs Your Daddy Didn't Want You to Hear*."

Alta lay back on the bed and laughed softly, but Bucky was already absorbed in the rhythm of another tune. He closed his eyes and sang the opening lines to "Barbara Allen."

> *Was in the merry month of May*
> *When flowers were a-bloomin'*
> *Sweet William on his deathbed lay*
> *For the love of Barbara Allen*
> *Slowly, slowly she got up*
> *And slowly she went nigh him*
> *And all she said when she got there*
> *"Young man, I think you're dying"*

I thought about the song as Bucky played it. I never did understand that one. What did the guy in the song do for Barbara Allen, anyway, except roll over and die from heartache? Not the best plan to reel in the gals. Still, he got off easy.

It's all the things you do for Barbara Allen when you have to keep on living that will ruin you and wreck you and make you wish you were dead.

Then again, maybe it's about the power of suggestion; of what mere words and ideas can really do if you let them get hold of you. Poor sap works himself into such a state over dear Barbary Allen, and all she can do is waltz in and say "young man, I do believe you're dying." And I wonder, was that a simple statement of fact, of the inevitable course of fate? Or was it a command?

The guitar rang out a final coppery-sounding G-chord, and as it died out it gradually dawned on me that Buck had been singing the last part of the tune in another language. Somewhere English had transitioned to something, well, something *other*, and it had passed right along the edge of my pickled consciousness. My brain struggled to get the question to my lips—where on earth did Bucky learn to sing like that?

"That's nice," said Alta, and suddenly I came to, as if I had dozed off. The vague unease that had crept in blew away like a clutch of leaves caught in the wind.

"That's another old one," said Bucky. "An old, old one." He was back to talking and joking in English, and not a particularly sophisticated variety, at that. The thought of a redneck like Bucky crooning in some obscure and ancient tongue was the height of absurdity. That seemed like a good enough time to walk away from both Bucky and Alta, and the whiskey that was going to my head.

47

"I oughta be a sport," I said, standing up, "and give you kids some privacy." The room wobbled slightly as the blood rushed to my head.

"Good night, Mr. Cecil," said Bucky, smiling as he made small adjustments with the guitar's tuning keys. "Tell the rest of the boys we did good tonight."

Then he was singing rockabilly again, grinning through a few verses of Billy Lee Riley's recent novelty song about the "little green mens" doing the bop to "Flying Saucer Rock-and-Roll."

I walked back out into the cold, where the crisp air had already begun to cut and slice away at the fog swirling around my mind. Still, out there in the dark, the little green mens and the Soviet Spies and God only knows what could be crouching behind every bush. Then a bitter wind blew right through me, the fog lifted, and I shuffled back to my room.

A little later I stood at the bathroom mirror, and even through the streaks and grime I felt that things were looking up. I had traded my cowboy hats for a scalp full of pomade, and but for a few extra lines on my face I could pass for one of the new crop, a rocking hillbilly cat, born again at 33. New ideas were churning below the placid surface of those big brown eyes—dangerous ones, even. Maybe I could wait a few more months and see if I could turn this gig into the start of something extra. Might put together some of the words and licks I had been scratching out on bar napkins and hotel

48

stationary, try pitching some songs for the next album. Hire myself out to some other young players; keep the good times rolling. Maybe even cut a few sides myself.

"Cecil, you seen Jim?" It was Junior, poking his head in the door.

"I thought he was with you," I said.

"Aw, hell. I lost track of him after the set," he said. Not a good sign. I could already feel a knot of tension pulling tight in my neck.

Out in the parking lot we ran into Dickie, looking jumpier than usual.

"Guys," he said, "I think Jim might be sick." He threw up a little, cupped his hands over his mouth, and took off like a rabbit.

Junior and I found Jim around the back of the motel, crawling around on his knees and elbows in the snow and making sounds like a lost dog. As Junior and I walked over, he collapsed in a heap.

"Jesus, Cec," said Junior, "what's he done to himself this time?"

"It could have been mixing reds and whiskey, or else he's got his hands on some morphine again."

Whatever it was, it was bad and getting worse by the second. Big Jim's skin had gone grey and clammy, and rubbing a handful of snow in his face didn't even make him flinch. Every few minutes, though, he would hack and choke like something was about to turn him inside-out.

Me and Junior looked at each other. I figure that Jim had nearly a hundred pounds on the

49

both of us put together. We were hoping that maybe the blizzard would kick up again, put some slick ice on the sidewalk so we'd have an easier time dragging Jim back to the room. We both looked skywards, hoping for absolution. The clouds opened up a flurry of snowflakes, like a perfectly-cued horn section in a cool jump blues.

The change in the weather seemed to accomplish what a scoop of slush from the sidewalk could not, and Big Jim stirred again. He sat up, eyes squinting into the night.

"I could go for a dip in the pool," he said. At that, he stood up and peeled off his shirt, scratching his big belly like the cold was nothing.

Hell, we tried to stop him, but it was like a couple of saplings growing up around the tracks, thinking they could hold back a freight train. I was on one side and Junior was on the other, and Big Jim drug us alongside him as he made his way towards the motel swimming pool. The gate was locked and chained, and as Big Jim started to haul himself up over the fence, I braced for the sound of impact, of bone and meat smacking concrete. Instead, I heard the sound of a full-on cannonball breaking the icy water of the uncovered swimming pool.

Jim's head bobbed to the surface, and he started laughing. Not his usual belly laugh, but a scream that turned into a laugh, a laugh at the end of a hangman's rope. It echoed off the concrete and stucco as Jim dove down and swam little laps back and forth. We watched in horror as lights started to wink on all over the motel.

"Come on, Jim," I said, "It's as cold as a witch's titty out here. We need to get back to the room."

More splashing. More peals of crazed laughter, louder this time.

"Cec, I think we better get scarce," said Junior. A window opened up somewhere, and another sound joined the fray.

"Goddammit! Shut that asshole up!"

"Fuck you, buddy!" said Big Jim.

"That's it, I'm coming down there, and I'm going to kick somebody's ass!"

"Cec..."

The promise of a good fight was too much for Jim to pass up. He hauled himself out of the pool, sloshing out a couple gallons in his wake. He tried to jump the fence again, but beginner's luck had deserted him, and he busted his ass on the sidewalk. He lay there on his back like a Cadillac-clipped o'possum, still laughing, as the threats and curses rained down on us.

Me and Junior finally counted to three, lifted up under each of Jim's massive arms. He got the picture. He stood up and made like he was about to shoo us away, and then promptly vomited all over my new two-tone shoes.

That was where I got off of that particular merry-go-round; I walked back to the room, swearing and cussing and trying to kick the chunkier stuff off my poor shoes. Junior tried to lead Jim in the same general direction, but Jim ignored him and lumbered off towards the road.

Across from the hotel, Jim sat under a big pine tree, brooding. It looked like somebody had shaved a grizzly bear, left him out in the rain, soaking wet and miserable. But since we could see him from the doorway of our motel room, we decided the best thing to do was to let him sort it out for himself. Me or Junior would peek out there every few minutes, making sure he hadn't collapsed in the snow or tried to stretch out on the road. Although as I tried to salvage my leather shoes, I would have entertained the idea of letting a few trucks roll over him before we went out to help. Eventually he trudged back to the room. He didn't knock, we just heard the sound of his forehead smacking on the door. Junior let him in and he slept where he fell, just a few feet from the doorway.

In light of the way things eventually turned out for Jim, I probably sound like a heartless bastard, but believe me, we'd all been down that trail before. I guess we should have taken him to a hospital, but we knew what would have come of that—a hospital bill, and a very angry Big Jim. He probably would've demanded that the record company people pay for it, and gotten us all shit-canned.

That night was a long one. I woke up twice to Jim thrashing around like a drowning man, wailing an absolutely harrowing string of gibberish. Woke up a third time to the faint sound of laughter.

A quick look around confirmed that Big Jim was still parked where we'd left him, his belly rising and falling with each wheezing breath.

Junior was asleep in the other bed. I saw a flicker of movement at the window, lit with an unsettling mix of blues and reds from the "no vacancy" sign. It was enough to get me on my feet, but by the time I got to the window the only motion outside was from the quivering limbs of the bushes. There were smudges on the glass, though, and the there was enough of that strange purplish glow to see that there were a number of fresh footprints in the snow. In my dazed, half-awake stupor, I groped around the idea for a minute and then I figured they must have been some kids. A bunch of fans, and they must have been looking for Bucky's room, which was probably close enough to the truth.

But then, as I wiped the crust from my eyes and blinked at the rapidly disappearing footprints, something else piped up in the back of my mind. Those footprints, they were too soft around the edges. Kids must be nuts, I thought, to walk barefoot through the snow.

I yawned. That voice in the back of my head shut up, and I headed back to bed.

I think there are some things that the mind will overlook for its own sake. Because I could have looked closer, thought about what I was seeing. I could have counted the digits on those footprints, or held my hand up to those smudges on the glass, see if anything lined up. As it was, exhaustion settled in and covered my thoughts like the falling snow outside erased those strange prints. Or maybe I ought to go ahead and call them tracks. I could have figured things out then, maybe even done some good. But I was too fried from the nightly grind, from the noise, and from the headache of dealing with Jim.

Looking back, though, it was an ill omen. Our bad times were just getting started.

Four:
"I'll outrun the devil on judgement day..."

"Cecil, I need somebody to talk to."

Alta's voice shocked me out of a daze that the black coffee in front of me had failed to lift.

"I mean, if that's okay with you." My face must have said it all. I didn't mean to shoot such a sour look. She snuck up on me, I suppose, both literally and by the nature of her request. Why would she be coming to me, her boyfriend's over-the-hill sideman, to confide anything?

I tried to sit up a bit straighter in the red vinyl booth. She had caught me feeling old and sorry for myself, I guess, which is not the face you want to show to somebody so young who already has a record deal.

"Oh, no problem at all, Alta. Fire away." I took another sip of coffee through my tired, half-assed grin.

Alta took a moment to purse her lips, and a line of worry—could've been the first, for all I knew—creased her forehead.

"It's Bucky," she said. "He's been saying things in his sleep."

"Okay," I said. I could already feel my smile starting to slip. "What kind of things?"

55

"Actually, I can't say. Not exactly. See, it doesn't sound like English to me."

"Well, I'm not exactly an expert translator. Know a little bit of Spanish. Know an even littler bit of Creole French. Past that I'm afraid I might not be much good to you."

"It's hard to tell what it is, but I don't think it's either of those."

"Well…" My thoughts trailed off. She was playing with an unused fork, tapping it nervously on the table-top.

"Cecil, do you know much about speaking in tongues?"

"Well, when I was a kid they had me play in church. Baptist, you know; my momma's church. But now and again I'd be loaned out, you might say, to go play for different congregations. They drove me a couple of times to a shabby Pentecostal church out in the middle of nowhere, sat me down at a raggedy pump organ, and had me play for hours while people wriggled on the floor and spoke nonsense."

"And what did you think?"

"It made me think I needed to get out of the churches and into the bars, where it's safer."

"Well," said Alta, "my Daddy brought us up stricter than boot camp, until people started complimenting my singing in the choir. Then he got the dollar signs in his eyes. But I seen one or two ladies from our church starting crying and carrying on during the services, working themselves up until they nearly swooned away. It kind of shakes you up to see it."

I thought, but did not say, that most church

ladies of that sort likely needed a shake, a rattle, and a roll to get all of that mess out of their system.

"But now I'll wake up some nights and Buck will be making the most awful sounds, and tossing back and forth so bad that he's nearly rolled out of the bed. And the worst of it is, sometimes he'll have his eyes wide open, and nearly bugging out of his head."

She tapped a nervous beat out on the tabletop.

"I'll try to wake him up, and all I'll get out of him is a string of something that sounds like he's trying to talk, only I can't understand any of it. Not a word. Then he'll stop—it's like he'll finally see me, even though I've been right in front of his face the whole time."

"Geez, kid," I said. She had a little glaze of tears in her eyes, and suddenly I felt lost. What could I do for a scared, barely grown child like her?

"Oh Cecil! They always used to tell us that the Lord could speak through people, sometimes. And I believed it, until I didn't anymore, like when I came to Nashville and saw a little more of the world than I knew, and all of that stuff suddenly seemed awful ignorant. But it's almost like something gets ahold of Bucky every so often, and I just don't know—"

She had pulled herself back together, wiping the tears from her eyes before they could roll down her pale cheeks. But she was still tap-tap-tapping on the table, and the way the booth was shaking I could tell her leg was jumping like she was working the pedal on a Singer sewing machine.

"The things he says, I don't recognize the words, but the tone of his voice! It sounds like—why, it sounds like a warning!"

In Louisiana we played our show live on the radio, meaning that aside from the crowd at hand we had reached people as far as 50,000 watts could travel. I imagined our beat drifting through the cattails, our guitar and piano licks hanging from trees like peat moss, and then Bucky's strange voice reaching out for new ears. It was a weird time in the swamps that night, I'll bet.

Bucky was riding high after the show, signing autographs and meeting new fans that hung on his every word. The man from the record company was there once again, sporting a nervous grin. Several radio stations were spinning our latest 45, and not just in the southeast, either. It seemed like Bucky, while not paying out in Elvis money, might be getting somewhere after all.

Meanwhile, I had been watching Jim like a hawk, trying to stave off the inevitable fuck-up that would get us all thrown out of the band. He was hanging in there, but his face was turning progressively redder by the end of the set each night. So when I saw the man from the record company waiting backstage, I immediately assumed the worst.

He was talking to a second man, who I also took for a record company employee. The other man, who I learned later went by Mr. Goe, couldn't have been taller than five foot, and he wore a pork-pie hat and dark sunglasses, even though it was already nighttime. He had a thick scarf that he wrapped around his face, where most of the remaining real estate was taken up by a gin-blossomed nose.

Mr. Goe was gesturing across the room at Bucky, and saying something to Mr. Kirby that made him look like he had just absorbed a particularly sharp blow to the groin. I was temporarily relieved. It looked like me and Jim weren't the ones in trouble this time. As he approached us, Mr. Kirby's rage was directed squarely at Bucky.

"Goddammit, Buck," he said, "we're all in deep shit now. How ignorant could you be?"

"I don't know," said Bucky, eyeing Mr. Goe. "What in hell you're talking about, sir."

"Don't act dumb. That 'aw shucks' country-boy horseshit isn't fooling me. You better come clean."

"Mr. Kirby," said Buck, "I don't have no idea what you're carrying on about."

"All right," said Kirby, lowering his voice, "I'll give you a hint. This man here says that you and him have business together. A management contract, of which you are in breach. A recording contract, of which you are also in breach. Good God, son, what were you thinking?"

He produced a handkerchief from his pocket, and began to dab the sweat from his forehead.

"I feel like the new groom," he said, "who

returns from his honeymoon with a bad case of the clap."

Things got heated after that. The argument between Mr. Kirby and Bucky continued all the way through the ride to the hotel and up to Mr. Goe's room. The rest of us were left behind, which at the time I much appreciated. Something about Mr. Goe gave me the creeps. As Bucky told us later, Goe didn't speak a word until they arrived back at his hotel room, where he produced a faded stack of papers and spread them out on the bed. There, to Bucky and Kirby's horror, was a comprehensive contract that detailed one Buchanan E. Bennett, and his relationship to Goe's management company. It was dated a good two or three years before Bucky had started recording for Mr. Kirby. And, worst of all, it bore Bucky's signature in many places, in his very own graceless scrawl.

"Good lord, Buck," said Mr. Kirby, standing outside the hotel room, "I don't blame you for trying to get out from under that deal. You'd never see a penny from that man."

Bucky maintained that he had never signed those documents, had never even seen this Mr. Goe before tonight. Mr. Kirby had a few more choice words, but he put them on hold, Bucky said, while he tried to go back and see if there was any way to wriggle out from under this. It might be expensive, but perhaps if they were all very lucky they could buy out Mr. Goe's contract.

Bucky joined us back in mine and Jim's hotel

60

room, along with Alta and the rest of the band. We all sat and watched Bucky pace back and forth. He kept repeating over and over that this was all a big scam, that those papers were fake, and that he had never seen Goe before in his life.

Well, I could believe him on the first two. But I had seen the look on Bucky's face earlier. That wasn't a case of the creeps or an uneasy suspicion, that was outright fear. Fear that had probably come from some prior experience. But maybe Bucky had his reasons for hiding the past. Plenty of people did. Who could turn down a fresh start in a brand new world like this?

It was about an hour or two later when we heard from Mr. Kirby. He called instead of stopping by the room, which already seemed like a bad sign.

"Well, I've talked him into letting us finish out the tour. Then we'll have to start the negotiations for real."

"Mr. Kirby," said Bucky, "There ought not to be any negotiations—we need to get a judge or somebody to tear all his phony papers up. Hell, what he needs is a good ass-whupping."

"Buck, it don't work like that. You need to face the facts. You cocked up this whole thing, and it's going to be expensive to fix. Best thing you can do is keep playing, making money, and make sure that the higher-ups at the company feel that you're worth the expense."

Bucky didn't say a word. The curl of his lip said it all.

"Remember that," said Kirby. "Now, you

boys be ready, we've got an early and a late show tomorrow. I'm going to try to get some rest, sleep off this whole mess. It's like to make me ill."

"We'll talk about all of this later, Buck."

"You bet we will," said Bucky. He slammed the receiver into the phone so hard the plastic cracked.

When I finally found sleep that night, it was fitful and restless, and something awful plagued me in what passed for a dream. I have a few recurring ones, anyway, and I've learned to recognize the anxieties they leave behind, same way some fellas can track wild game from the impressions in the ground.

First one is a dream of a lousy gig. I mean, the worst my brain can conjure. Bad crowd, no whiskey, pedals and keys sticking and breaking, and the bandleader—always Carl Weber at his meanest—riding my ass. And no Jim to watch my back. A clutch of sour faces crowd around the closes table, topped with black bowlers that look just a little too tight. I can't hear them, but I can see their eyes flash as one of them gestures towards me. They want to cut my pinkies off, or perhaps empty the chamber of a pistol right beside my good ear. I can wake up from this dream and shake it off with a few minutes of pacing and a glass of water. I've had so many bad gigs that a little medley of the worst of them can't do squat-all to me. Most nights.

My second dream goes back much farther. I'm no more than fifteen, and I'm back home with my Aunt Nora. Something terrible is happening outside, and she has both her arms wrapped tight around me. They're the arms of a farmer's oldest daughter; fleshy and sun-damaged, but underneath the muscles are stronger than I ever realized. I can't tell anymore if she's trying to reassure me, or if she's holding me back. Or maybe she just needs to hold on bad as me.

We're watching a crowd of people drag our next-door neighbor out of his house. He is a tall, lanky man, his hair dark and nearly as thick as his accent, which is definitely not native to the South. Earlier that day there was an argument in town, or maybe not. Maybe he whistled at somebody or let his gaze linger a little too long. Maybe money was involved somehow. Maybe it was just that he owned a store in town and most people there did not. I can no longer recall the motives of the gathering crowd—and I wonder how many of them can say the same thing. But I do remember what happens next. The men on either side of my neighbor forced him down to his knees. He begins to plead in broken English, then he prays in his own language, which whips the crowd into an even greater frenzy. Soon his skin is shiny with the tar, and Nora pulls my head down as one of the men who teaches me Sunday school walks forwards holding a brightly burning torch.

This dream, too, I can shake off, but not without some effort, and usually another drink, whiskey instead of water. I remind myself that this is also based on memories, ones that I put in the rearview a long time ago. It's still the same rotten world, of course, but not all of it has to follow after what happens in the backwoods of Georgia.

Last dream is one that has been with me since I was a small child. It's the original nightmare, the primal fear, and it's never easy to shake. I'm home in this dream, too, only I can't find Nora, and I walk back and forth in the house calling her name. I hear something outside, something that might be a woman's screams, and I step out on the porch to try and find the source. As I bound down the front steps, somehow I don't realize that most of the ground in front of the house has collapsed in on itself, leaving a massive sinkhole. I start to fall, but I reach out just in time to grab ahold of something, and I hang there, trying to claw my way back up to safety. Then I feel the pull, an increasing weight, and a feeling like molasses being poured over me, slowing my frantic flailing. It won't let me up, won't let me fall, and my struggle for life ends up more like a comical wallowing on the edge of the abyss. After what feels like hours, I let go, wanting at last to fall, to end the nightmare. My descent is so slow as to be imperceptible, and I pray for the darkness, to be enveloped by it. But the sinkhole opens wider, like a great mouth, and I can see farther and farther below. And there's something moving in the dark down there…

The next morning I woke up feeling like a sailor on a ship that had been too long at sea. My clothes itched and I was in need of a good meal. But diner food and coffee would have to do.

Soon Jim, Alta, Junior and I sat in a booth. Buck sat out in the Cadillac, brooding. Dickie helped him. The coffee arrived, black as road tar and not near as tasty. Jim only took half a cup, and then filled it up the rest of the way with water. This was his concession to the fresh ulcer that was gnawing at his guts.

We sat in silence for what seemed like a long time.

"Hell of thing," said Junior. "I'd hate to think to ride is over already."

"Wouldn't be the first kid to go down under a pile of lawyers."

Alta glared at me.

"Sorry, Alta."

"When I was starting out," said Alta, "my daddy had signed some awful deals. By the time he had the sense to realize what he'd done, it was too late. But he tried. Went with my brother and cousin, threatened to beat somebody's ass."

"What happened?" asked Junior.

"They broke his fingers."

All the musicians at the table flinched like somebody had threatened to take off their nuts with a butter knife.

"Don't think Mr. Kirby is going to be good for much intimidation," I said. "He's going to let us finish out this round of shows, then he's going to cut us all loose. Leave Bucky to flap in the wind. Sorry, Alta."

"Oh, it's his own damn fault," she said. "He's still only telling me half of the truth. I don't know what he's hiding, but I'll bet it's a whopper."

"Well, Miss Alta," said Jim, "what do you say? You in need of an old hillbilly bass player?"

"Hell, Jim, you know they wouldn't let me cut a record with you fellas. Next time I go in the studio I'll have to use a crowbar to make my way through all the back-up singers and string players. If you really want to find out what it's like to have the record people stick a corncob up your ass, try being a woman singing rock-n-roll."

Jim laughed so hard he got to coughing. He took another swig of watery coffee and said, "Hey, at least you still have some kind of career. We'll be back to scrabbling for back-up gigs. And Bucky's days in the biz could be numbered, after all this mess."

"I know," said Alta, looking out the window. "The poor fool."

That night the show had taken on a different feel. The joy of discovery was gone, but between Bucky's troubles and the ache in Big Jim's guts we had more than enough fuel for another kind of fire. Before the beat had been light and effervescent, no matter how frantic the tempo. Tonight we played a slow number, and the swish of Dickie's brushes on the snare drum sounded like a man shuffling his way to the gallows.

Out in the audience, Mr. Kirby and Mr. Goe sat and watched. Kirby looked like he had tried to sleep off his troubles and hadn't caught a wink. Mr. Goe leaned forward in his seat, his long fingers intertwined, one leg dangled over the other. His body language was that of the cat who ate the canary, but his face, what little of it could be seen, showed not even a hint of a smile.

After the show, Bucky tried to talk to Mr. Kirby, but it was pointless. He was impossible to separate from Mr. Goe now, and it seemed like the very sight of Bucky only sickened him further. It was back to the rooms, in a smaller motel that night.

Bucky was pacing again, putting everybody on edge.

"This is a bunch of horseshit," said Bucky, "They can't do me like this—treat me like an old plow-horse. They're trying to work this thing to death, ship me off to the glue factory."

Jim and Junior were passing the time with a card game. Junior looked up from his hand at Bucky, giving him a well-rehearsed stink eye.

"Buck," he said, "there's something about all this that doesn't square up. We all figure that you know this Goe character from somewhere. It's not that any of us would blame you for trying to get out from under that old buzzard, but..."

"I told you fellas," said Buck, hands on the sides of his head, "I don't know that guy from Adam!"

There was a general murmur around the room. Even Dickie acted like he thought Bucky was full of it.

"Just let it out, brother," said Big Jim, "we've

all got our troubles. What are you running from?"

Bucky stood by the window now, looking out into the darkness as if it were pressing in, about to crack the glass and pour on top of him.

"There's plenty."

Mister Cecil, I told you before how I never knew my daddy. Well, all I ever knew of mama was that she went crazy before I was old enough to walk. They locked her away in one of those state hospitals for trying to dunk me in kerosene and light me up. It sounds horrible, I know, but it's the truth.

Grandma wasn't near as gone as mama was, and she had her good points, but she talked nonsense all the time about mama and daddy. Said that mama had slept with a man that wasn't just a cheat and a drunk; to hear Grandma tell it, he wasn't a man at all. That's why things turned out the way they did—not just with mama, but other things too. Grandma told me I had a twin brother that was stillborn.

Grandma's family had come from Ireland about two hundred years ago, but they had spent most of those years up in the mountains, and they kept the old ways with them. Grandma believed in the old stories, ghosts and fairies and such. So when she saw that baby brother of mine born all dead and withered up, and me just as healthy and pink and fat as can be, it rattled her poor old brain. And when mama went crazy like she did, ranting about her baby being some kind of monster, Grandma's ears started a-

twitching and her mouth started working and she figured she knew exactly what was going on.

But it wasn't nothing that ever made a damn lick of sense. She kept changing her mind, telling the story different each time. Told me my daddy was some kind of fairy-critter, squattin' in the woods. Laid with my mama one night and gave her those twins, but all that wicked fairy blood ended up in my brother, so he never made it. Or maybe they came and took my brother out of my mama while she was sleeping one night, and left me alone in her belly with a clutch of soggy branches and creek mud.

Or maybe they were still out there. Still after me, a child that they figured they had a claim on, because of who my daddy was. That's what she finally decided on, as we hustled from town to town.

Don't you see? My family was nuts, a bunch of looney-tunes down to the dark roots, but I never knew it until I got older. Me and grandma, we never stayed anywhere for long. She put me to working, or more often to stealing, just to keep us both fed. Never been to school like I should, just had Grandma filling my head up with haints and bogies and a bunch of other horseshit. I never had a real home, never was loved by anyone healthy or happy enough to make me feel like anything other than a no-good hillbilly bastard. And when I got old enough to know it, I took off. I left Grandma to howl and rave at herself and hit the road. Fell into singing along the way, but I never really stopped running.

69

So this Mr. Goe comes in, and I don't know him—but I maybe do, after all. He's that look I always got from Grandma, the one that let me know I'll be peering over my shoulder for the rest of my life. I don't know if somebody in the family put him up to this, now that I'm making records and singing on the radio. Somebody could be trying to blackmail me. All I know for sure is when the dates we've got booked run out, Goe is going to make sure that the running stops. And that scares me.

All this time I've been trying to leave the past behind. I got spun out into the world with nothing but a bad name and a head filled up with nonsense, and all I've ever wanted was to find a place for myself. I figured it might as well be the stage; I don't have no fear of it, see, because everyday life is a show for me. Trying to pass myself off as somebody better.

They kept us to the Southeast on the last leg of the tour, hitting places that we'd played twice before, and filling the nights in-between with gigs in places we'd passed over the first time around. There were no more package shows and big revues on the schedule, no more sense of triumph, just a bunch of tired musicians stretched out as thin as paper, and one rockabilly singer with an aura of doom so thick around him it threatened to suffocate us all.

The slouch was back, as if the guitar around his neck was made of solid concrete, and the little divot in Bucky's chin vanished as quickly as it had appeared. His face had gotten gaunt, and the old pox scars that had faded seemed to deepen anew.

Mr. Kirby and Mr. Goe were always there, hovering over Bucky like a couple of well-tailored vultures, inseparable. But Kirby was looking worse every day, as sallow as a hunk of spoiled cheese, and about as personable. Junior told me that he had watched them as we played one night, just staring at us with morbid curiosity from up in the balcony. Every few minutes Mr. Goe produced a flask and handed it to Kirby, who dutifully took a swig, looking sicker with every swallow. Junior said he never known Kirby to drink more than a thimble-full, even when he was working a deal. Strange. And Goe never taking a drop for himself, just offering the flask to Kirby again and again.

My own brush with Mr. Goe was just as sickening.

It was in the hallway of that night's hotel, which was roomier than usual, if you didn't mind the smell. I didn't at the time, though I can't say I wasn't more than a little drunk. Whiskey will often steel the nerves when the courage runs out. But the show had been a good one that night; the boys and I had played like fire while Bucky sang with a gospel singer's conviction. If we couldn't put a brave face on what was going to happen once the tour was over, at least we could squeeze every last drop from these final nights.

So I must have been walking a little too tall for my own good, because Mr. Goe took it upon

71

himself to cut me down. I saw him shuffling down the hall towards me, and I tried to avoid his gaze the best I could. It seemed to burn uncleanly even behind the tinted glass of those shades he wore.

"I knowed your daddy, boy," he said as we passed. It was barely above a whisper, in that strange, muffled voice of his, but it felt like someone had slugged me in the gut with an axe-handle.

I turned to face him, blood already burning in my cheeks. He was standing there, bundled up under all that heavy wool and cotton, even with the air as hot and sticky as a swamp in that hotel. I was starting to sweat just looking at him, but it was from the rage he was trying to stoke as much as anything.

"Yessir, Mr. Cecil, met him right near the very end."

"You shut your goddamn mouth," I said, but it wasn't backed up by much. Suddenly my whiskey courage had gone watery and weak.

"Well, it was maybe a little more second-hand, now that I remember it. I knowed the tree, you see, where they..."

And he made a motion with his hand, pulling a rope around and around then lifting it up high. And my own hands wanted to make a fist, to knock the little man halfway down the hall. But that would mean touching him, however briefly, and something about that sent a wave of revulsion up my spine and back down again.

"Hey," said a voice from over my shoulder. It was Bucky, looking even more disheveled than me, but with a glint of anger flashing in his eyes. "Leave him alone."

He walked towards us, but the closer he got the more it seemed like that anger was being cut with fear. He looked as pale as I've ever seen anyone, even worse than Big Jim when he turned the color of a fish-belly and threw up on my shoes.

"Whatever he says, Cecil, it's worse than lies. He's like a sewer."

Mr. Goe regarded the both of us from behind his dark glasses, and he chuckled to himself. He looked old and frail, but there was something else there, making that very age and slightness take on a dreadful power. He suddenly seemed ancient, and implacable.

"My, my. Don't the two of you make a pair." And then there was that chuckle again, from somewhere deep within. And then he called Bucky a hillbilly, and he called me a name that I've heard far too often to want to repeat here. It's bad enough to hear the people around you use it—even some very old friends of mine. I haven't heard it referring to myself so much, but then, once is more than enough.

With that Mr. Goe turned and left, taking some of the revulsion with him but leaving the fear and rage to hang in the air like the stale funk that clung to the walls. Bucky watched as he walked off, then his eyes met mine.

"Cecil..."

But I stormed off, and I left Bucky alone with the fear.

That night, I went to take another look in the bathroom mirror, but the younger man I had seen before had deserted me. This time, all I could see were a pair of tired eyes and three-day stubble. I turned on the faucet, gathered up a handful of water, and splashed it on my face.

"You look like cold dogshit, boy."

In the mirror I saw someone standing behind me, and my eyes nearly popped out. It was Carl Weber, my old bandleader.

"Jesus, Carl," I said, "I thought you were still in prison—"

I wheeled around, wondering how in the hell he had gotten in. But I only saw a grimy light switch and a piece of mint-green wallpaper that was starting to curl up at the edge.

I did a double take and looked back at the mirror. There, in the mirror, and only in the mirror, was an image of Carl Weber. He was dressed in his best Nudie suit: teal and orange patterns covered in purple rhinestone half-notes. His tallest cowboy hat loomed overhead.

"Don't change the subject, now. You remember what we used to say about you?"

"I must be going crazy..."

"You? Hell! We used to say that about Jimbo, that fat fuck. Oh no. You, we used to pass off as 'one-quarter Greek.'" Carl coughed up a dark chuckle. "Why, you're no more Greek than the man in the moon."

"Shut up, Carl." His smell had crept into the room with me; a sickening mix of stale sweat and gin.

"Hey, don't get touchy. All I'm saying is, we

figured there were plenty of reasons why you never met your daddy. Yes, we all guessed why he must have wanted to make dust when your mama turned out to be pregnant."

He was right, the son-of-a-bitch. Those reasons turned up on my face and in my hair, only they were just a whisper; a muted rumor that my Aunt Nora drug us across three counties to shake loose.

"Shut the fuck up, Carl."

Carl just smiled, his teeth rotten from years of sucking on chewing tobacco.

"Yeah," he said, "you probably could teach Bucky a thing or two about passing."

I put a fist through the mirror, cracking it in a dozen places.

"Watch your mitts, son," said a dozen gaudily-dressed Carl Webers. "What good are you without that strong left hand?"

Stupid stupid stupid. Blood welled up around the glass in my hand.

"Think about all those kids sorted out on the floor and the balcony. I wonder what those colored kids saw when they looked at your not-at-all-Greek ass sitting up there playing rockabilly. I already know what the white kids saw—nobody, nobody at all."

My right hand shook as I tried to pull a shard a glass out of my left. Only thing it did was slice up my fingertips real good.

"Seems, though, like maybe you've been thinking different lately. After all, this whole rock-and-roll thing hits, and suddenly all bets are off—hillbillies are getting rich playing rhythm and blues, black men are writing country songs for white teenagers, all things are selling to all kinds of people, at long-everloving-last."

I grabbed a hotel towel, and used it to pull out the biggest piece of glass. Bad idea; the wound started to spurt uncontrollably, soaking the towel in blood. Any pressure on the wound would just drive the rest of the glass deeper into my flesh.

"We all knew you had some half-assed designs on the spotlight, Cecil, but it was good sense that kept you in the background. Though now, maybe you figured you could stand the glare after all. That's just a pipe dream, boy. There's only so far you can climb with a boogie beat and a pair of two-tone shoes. Sooner or later, the past catches up with everybody."

I gritted my teeth. I couldn't see what I was doing to my hands for all the blood. I turned the water on in the sink and held my hands under it, causing searing pain to wash over me. Crimson trailed from my wounds and spiraled down the drain, looking like the bright swirls in peppermint candy.

"That's the way it has to be. You play a fair piano, but you're strictly a side-man, Cecil. But you're better off for it." A brief look of impossible agony danced across Carl's face. Suddenly he was dressed in filthy grey prison clothes, his bald head shining like it was covered in axle grease. He started to fade from the mirror, slowly. "That spotlight isn't just bright, boy. It's deadly."

I slumped down in the shower, picking glass

out of my knuckles and feeling like a fever was boiling all the meat off my bones. Blood pulsed out of my hands, but weaker than before. The world came tumbling off its axis, and a dark sea of red was the last thing that I saw.

I woke up next morning to the sound of someone banging on the bathroom door. I jerked up, knocking my head on the inside of the shower stall so hard it almost put me back under. I looked down, expecting to see my ruined hands and blood-soaked clothes, but I didn't have a scratch. The mirror was intact, but I hung a towel over it anyway. Couldn't trust it anymore.

It was Big Jim banging on the door, but instead of looking for a place to unload his whiskey breakfast, he came grasping a newspaper in his shaking hands. Junior was right behind him.

"It's Carl," said Jim. His face was flush and his voice cracked when he spoke.

"Carl," I said, heart suddenly racing again. "What about Carl?"

"His heart gave out on him," said Junior. "He died in his cell last night."

So who was my daddy? A black man, maybe with some mixed blood himself? Creole or half-Cherokee, maybe, but surely not light enough to go unnoticed by a lynch mob, especially when they figured out he had been passing the time with some blue-eyed farmer's daughter. He either made it or he didn't, I suppose, and if Nora knew anything about him she figured I was better off without it. It was likely he worked a plow or swung a hammer for a living, like most people I knew in Georgia, but I wonder sometimes if he could have been a musician.

I'm sure he did what he had to do to get by. Just like me. I made my name, such as it is, playing with the likes of Carl, but I can't say I'm going to miss the man or his sorry, ignorant ilk. Guys like that will cut you down every time without even knowing why, their meanness lashing out like the lingering reflexes from a corpse. They won't ever let you forget how the game shakes out, or what becomes of anybody on the losing end. You are who they say you are. They've built up a wall a hundred feet high, and they all get to act like it doesn't exist. But a long time ago I said to hell with it, and I acted like it didn't exist either. That much has taken me places my daddy could never have gone; places he probably would've been scared shitless to have been. It hasn't always been easy, but it's the life I've chosen. Though Christ almighty, there's such a price to pay.

Five:

"Where the rain never falls and the sun never shines..."

That last leg of the tour was as crooked as a dog's; seemed it was somebody's whim that we get back to Memphis by going through the mountains. The gigs got smaller and more depressing, in dives so far out in the sticks that we were probably the first (and last) they ever heard of rock-and-roll. Alta had joined us again, to try and see Bucky through to the end. He was drinking like a fish, and looked so awful that I was afraid he might have managed to sneak some of Big Jim's brand of poison by us.

I was exhausted from the pace of the last eight months or so—not just from playing and traveling, but from keeping an eye on Jim, not to mention steering clear of any more surprise run-ins with Goe. Paranoia tainted everything, including the whiskey I used to drive it away. Even the piano made me wary; I kept having nasty dreams of razor blades hidden between the keys, and sick laughter that blossomed when the blood started flowing.

The motel that night couldn't have been more cramped if they had tried to squeeze us all in a matchbox. As the record company's faith in Bucky waned, so too did the size and quality of our accommodations. The whole band was expected to share one room, including Bucky and Alta, while Mr. Kirby and Mr. Goe stretched out in the relative comfort of an adjoining suite. We sat up talking and griping and playing cards for a few extra hours, knowing that the whole gig was as good as over when we got back to Memphis.

Turns out, we didn't have to wait that long.

It was close to 4 AM when Alta shook me awake. All of us in the band had taken the floor that night, leaving the bed to Bucky and Alta in our last attempt at chivalry. I rolled over, my back already aching, and sat up slowly. Alta looked paler than usual.

"Cec, Buck's gone. I turned over and nearly rolled off the bed. He must have snuck out, and I think he's about to do something stupid—"

"And you figured he'd need help from the experts," said Big Jim. He was already awake, a light glaze of sweat across his face and blood shattering the whites of his eyes.

"I'm just afraid of what he'll try to pull. He's just thinking like a drifter again. He doesn't know how short of a leash they've got him on. If he runs off with the Cadillac, they'll say he stole it. If he gets in a fight with somebody, they'll let him sit in jail while they carve up his contract like a roasted turkey."

Just then the sound of screaming from the next room seemed to tell what option Bucky had taken.

Only problem was, it was Bucky doing the screaming.

It only took two kicks for Big Jim to bust the door down, but the scene inside the other room had already turned grisly. Bucky had initiated negotiations with a switchblade, but it seemed like Mr. Goe had made one hell of a counter-offer. Bucky lay sprawled on the floor, his own blade dangling from his side. Mr. Goe stood over him, reaching down with arms that seemed too long for such a short man. He held Bucky's face with a delicate touch, but it made Bucky grimace and snarl with raw pain. He was doing something terrible to Bucky, but we just couldn't understand it right away. As he struggled beneath Mr. Goe's spidery fingers, Bucky's skin seemed more fragile than it should. Pliable, like wet clay.

Alta let out a brain-rattling scream. I guess she could see it a little sooner than the rest of us.

At the sound of her scream, Mr. Goe cast aside his hat, his scarf, his sunglasses, and his jacket, and any illusion of humanity instantly dissipated.

The leathery creature that stood there walked on two legs like a man, but it was clear that some serious mojo had been employed for it to keep up the ruse. A baggy neck emerged from its narrow shoulders and held up a monstrous nose, but there were only wrinkles of flesh where the eyes would have been, and at first glance, no mouth to be seen. Pointed, bat-like ears twitched, and sparse hair bristled

81

everywhere. The thing rubbed its long fingers together, like a housefly in the ecstasy of a powerful hunger. It made a sighing sound, and part of its belly opened when it did, revealing two needle-sharp rows of teeth.

"Fellows," said the belly-mouth, "I've nearly collected on my debt."

"Help," said Bucky, as Mr. Goe's elongated toes curled around his throat.

Jim lunged at Goe, but the creature moved like grass in high wind, and Jim went tumbling across the room. Mr. Goe seized a fistful of Bucky's hair and started towards the door. Sheer revulsion started to push me and Alta away.

"You've come for me," said Bucky, "Just like you came and took my twin brother."

"Not quite," said Mr. Goe, in a soft, nauseating purr. "We've come to take you back."

A blast of gunfire went off to my left, taking half of my hearing along with it. I looked over and saw Alta standing with a smoking .38. She had fired nearly point-blank, but her hands had been shaking, and the bullet had only clipped one of the thing's ears. It let out a shriek, then it stormed past Alta and me, Bucky still trailing behind in its grip.

Outside the air bit like a starving dog and the crickets had gone silent. The only sounds were the curses and cries that came from Bucky as his back was scraped raw on the sidewalk. Alta and I tried to grab a foot, a leg, anything—but Goe moved fast for someone pulling a body twice his size. I managed to wrap an arm around Bucky's left leg, but as soon as I did, I felt my stomach turn. Bucky's leg felt all wrong—it started to give like a thick piece of rubber, and the shock made me let go just as Bucky uttered a feral howl of pain.

Alta gave me a look that made me think that she might shoot me for letting go, and then we heard Big Jim's voice.

"Catch this, you sonofabitch!"

Big Jim appeared and hurled the tire iron from the Cadillac, a big crossed-steel projectile that scored a direct hit and knocked Mr. Goe ass-over-ankles.

Jim stood over Bucky and Mr. Goe, both trying to make it to their feet. The horror that had served as a head for Mr. Goe was even more repulsive now, the bone and cartilage caved-in on one side. It struggled to stand, the teeth in its belly gnashing, but Jim was ready to finish the job, crimson streaks of rage pulsing under his cheeks.

That's when the rest of them came.

From somewhere at the edge of the woods the padding of bare feet sounded like the first drops of a rainstorm. They came from under the ground, from under the rocks and from where the tree-roots twisted into the dirt. They ran at Big Jim, clung to him, crawled and hopped and oozed all over him.

There were things that looked like Mr. Goe's distant relations, only scaled down to a few inches. Some looked more human, but their extra limbs, wings, and cilia gave them away as much as their size. There were half-animal creatures; toad-men, snail-men, and mole-men. There were things made of moss and bark, with tiny rows of pine-needle teeth. There were laughing sprites and hissing kobolds and things from so deep underground they had never needed eyes. They came by twos and threes, then by dozens, and soon there was a wave washing over Jim, a flood that kicked and howled and bit.

Big Jim waded into them like he was back on Omaha Beach. He swatted and stomped and flung their tiny, elastic bodies to the ground, some of them still holding bits of hair and skin in their teeth. He picked the tire iron back up, swinging it back and forth and mashing the critters to hamburger under his boots.

A squat grey thing with a head like a stag beetle hopped up on a rock next to where big Jim was turning his buddies into pulp. It pulled out a stick with a crudely-cut stone lashed to it and raised it over its shoulder. The stone came down on Jim's calf, leaving a gash that started to weep thick sheets of blood. Jim let out a snarl of choked agony as he snatched the grey thing up, its tiny axe clattering on the rock as Jim started to squeeze his massive hand. A pair of beady black eyes bulged and then popped out of the thing's head as Jim crushed its leathery body. You could hear it laughing hysterically the whole time.

Alta emptied her gun, trying to keep the monsters at bay. I gave a swift kick at anything that clamored too near. Through all the chaos, I spotted Mr. Goe dragging Bucky off into the woods.

"Look," I said, "There he goes."

The thing that we knew as Mr. Goe ambled through the forest, dragging Bucky by his hair over rocks and sticks and mud. Alta and I ran after, arms up while a hundred tiny claws snatched at our clothes. As we got closer, we could see that Mr. Goe wasn't just dragging Bucky, he was pulling him out of shape, his neck and limbs stretching like overheated taffy.

Mr. Goe reached a clearing where a cluster of stumps and mossy stones formed a loose circle, and by the time he did, Bucky no longer resembled the man we had played behind these past months.

What gasped and choked and bled there at Mr. Goe's feet was now only marginally less grotesque than Goe himself. Most of Bucky's clothes had been torn to shreds as he had been pulled through the bushes and rocks, and he was covered in bloody slashes everywhere his bare skin showed. He was filthy with dirt and leaves, but that wasn't the worst of it. Twigs hadn't just gotten stuck in Bucky's hair, they had taken root there, producing fresh green buds at the tips. Kudzu vines grew from any cuts or scratches deep enough to drink from. Grey toadstools were sprouting on his skin.

A couple of the smaller creatures skipped and danced around Bucky and Mr. Goe, pulling Bucky's ears and eyelids out of shape and babbling strange chants. One of them capered a little too close to Mr. Goe; he snatched up the greasy pixie and stuffed it into his belly-mouth with a satisfied grunt.

Alta took a good look at what had become of Bucky and broke down crying. If she had still had a bullet left, I'm sure she would have used it on him. His distended limbs twitched helplessly, the bones deformed, their muscles stretched too thin to support them. His eyes rolled back, crossed and uncrossed, veered off in different directions. Bucky tried to speak, but Mr. Goe reached down and gave his tongue a good twist, cutting off the words.

"He was probably going to say something pitiful, like 'save me' or 'help,'" said Mr. Goe. "Better to save him the embarrassment, don't you think?"

Then he saw how Alta was crying, and he smiled so big with his belly-mouth he looked like he was going to split in two. He was crawling with wicked delight.

"Or maybe," he said, "he was going to say 'I love you?' Maybe something half-assed noble, like 'run while you can?' There are so many possibilities."

Alta threw her gun in a rage, but Mr. Goe dodged it as gracefully as a dancer.

"Look at him, he's no good to you anymore. He'll never fool anyone now; he's lost the shape of a man for good. This is what happens to the ones who forget, the ones who try to get away. By the time we're done with him, he won't remember being anything more than a patch of slime under a rotted log."

And with that, Mr. Goe took a handful of

Bucky's hair once again. He dipped a toe into what looked like an old knot-hole in a hollowed-out stump, and then his whole body slid inside as easy as a hair into a bathtub drain. The smaller creatures followed him down, each holding a section of Bucky's warped limbs, feeding him into the stump until there was no one left in the clearing but me and Alta.

There was a cry from somewhere under the ground, with an echo that traveled far below, into what sounded like a honeycomb of chambers, just beneath the surface.

We ran. Big Jim was just wiping the paste and gore off when we made it back from the woods. Junior and Dickie were up, having watched with stunned disbelief from the window of our room. The whole thing had played out in a few minutes.

In the other hotel room, we found what had been Bucky's contract—now only a few strips of dried birch bark. Mr. Kirby was slumped in-between the bed and the wall, cold as a stone. His mouth was stuffed with leaves and twigs, and he had dropped the flask, which was only ever filled with brackish pond water.

The rest of the hotel seemed to be deserted—maybe all of the other guests and even the man at the front desk had been a part of it; maybe they had gotten crushed, in another form, by Big Jim's tire iron.

We found the keys to the Cadillac out on the sidewalk. They must have fallen out of Bucky's pocket. We drove and drove through the night, and we didn't stop until we reached a city, where all the ground and everything below it was pavement and concrete.

We ended up in Knoxville, shell-shocked, with no clear path ahead. People would come looking for Bucky, and for Mr. Kirby, who presumably had a family that didn't lurch around in the bowels of the earth. Junior and Dickie wanted to go to the police, Big Jim was ready to skip town and make for Mexico, and Alta sat on the hotel bed, clutching a Bible so hard I thought she'd tear it to shreds.

In the end it was Alta's people that kept us safe when they found Mr. Kirby's body. She was already a rising star by then, and whatever sordid details came out of her association with us were wiped clean by the hand of God and the Nashville recording industry. As far as anyone ever knew, Mr. Kirby drank himself to death in his hotel room, despondent over the impending loss of his prize discovery. Such an end was not uncommon in country music.

Alta herself headed back to Nashville, where she got born-again and ditched rockabilly for lily-white gospel and pop music. She never sang with the same fire, but her talent was still a rare and dazzling thing, so she sold more records than the rest of us ever dreamed of, and made so much money even the record company couldn't steal it all. Once she sent me a check with a dizzying number of zeros on it; an advance for playing piano on one of her records. I showed up and spent three days in a studio playing along to a click track, and if Alta was around she never let me know it. I understood completely. The handful of times the studio engineer let a little bit of her voice slip through the headphones I nearly shook to death. That was the last time I ever heard from her. From what you can read in the papers, it seems she married one of her producers after the hits gave out. As far as I know, they never had any children.

Junior and Dickie moved to Nashville and played together often, backing singers both slight and sublime, and even cut a few instrumental records with a bunch of other studio players. I half-heartedly tried to break into the same studio scene, but we rarely worked together anymore; if I was around the past wasn't quite so easy to ignore, and ignoring the past is something Nashville does even better than cut hit records.

Dickie is still around, only going by "Richie" now. Royalty payments keep him well-fed, but his sense of fashion stalled out sometime when muttonchops and wide collars were in. Junior passed away in his sleep some years ago, next to his wife of fifty years. His house in Nashville was filled with gold records and expensive guitars.

Big Jim also died in his sleep. In his case, though, it was after a night that included two busted taillights, three shots of morphine, a twenty-year-old hooker, a half-bottle of Johnny Walker, and one television set taken apart with a fire ax. He was 49 years old, going on seventeen and a half. I think about where he might be if he had lived as long as me, or even as long as Junior, and I shudder. He was spared from paying a drunk's wages in his old age, but he lived long enough to see his own vocation become obsolete (no electric bass for Big Jim), which is bad enough. Who can blame him for wanting to blot out the world?

Bucky Bennett's disappearance went mostly unnoticed. Unlike Buddy and Eddie and Ace, nobody wrote a death disc for Bucky; though I'm not entirely sure whether you could say he died then, a thought which gave me more sleepless nights than I care to count. Once, though, some vulture at the record company must of had a bright idea, and put out a final single. I nearly stomped the radio flat when I heard that voice coming out of the speakers, singing gibberish that suddenly didn't seem so agreeable anymore. Then again, maybe it wasn't the record company. Maybe somebody out there had decided to broadcast a special message just for me. I kept the radio off for a long time, and I tried not to think about it.

For a while I had to keep certain writers off my back; they all wore thick-rimmed glasses and mustaches right out of a walrus herd, and they all had a burning desire to pick at all the scabbed-over areas of my life. Not just mine, I'm sure, but anybody that had played their hands back in the early days of rock-and-roll and had come up losing. And believe me, there are plenty of losers. Even the greats from back then ended up crazy, in jail, or dead before their time. We all had a hand in creating this new, liberated world; we just didn't get to live in it.

I can tell you, though, if I had ever told them the truth about Bucky, they would have laughed my ass out of the room. Hell, maybe they did. I drank an awful lot for a long, long time.

Junior White's funeral was a regular record industry petting party; I could scarcely breathe for the volume of people who were there to reminisce and whack each other on the back and blather on about the old days. Jim's funeral had been attended by me and the mosquitoes. He was buried next to his daddy. Both times I watched the caskets get swallowed up by the earth and I thought, to hell with that. When I die they can cut me up, part me out, anything but stick me in the ground.

Now I've gotten old. Older than I ever planned for, though that's not saying much. I've outlived all my friends, or maybe I've just outlived the need for friends. I played until my hands twisted up with arthritis, then kept trying until I nearly crippled myself. Once upon a whiskey-soaked time I felt like music was keeping me young, but by the time I'd given it up the light patter of applause had started to sound like dirt raining down on a coffin lid.

I ran until my knees and my back went south; switched from running to walking, walking to limping. Now I figure I'd crawl if I hadn't ended up in this nursing home, where they hate my stubborn old ass and watch me like a hawk.

It's safe here, I think. All linoleum and painted concrete inside, the natural world quarantined into pitiful little window boxes full of limp pansies. No mole-tunnels or rabbit warrens or any other cleverly-disguised holes to hell. I think I may have gotten away.

But sometimes, I wake up at night with music ringing in my ears. Not the sound of slip-fingered piano licks or chopping guitar chords, but the voices from below. I hear Bucky's voice, and Mr. Goe's. Big Jim and Junior, too, and even my dear old dad's. They call to me and laugh.

I listen, and then I'm not so sure.

Acknowledgements

Thanks to Angie Price, who helped me chop this down for submission.

Many thanks to my family, especially my grandmother, for the stories (even if I've jumbled them all up now).

Thanks to everyone at 18thWall, for giving this slow-burner a place to catch fire.

R.I.P. to the great Nick Tosches, who wrote a beautiful line about Elvis that inspired this entire novella. There is no new thing under the sun.

DID YOU ENJOY WHAT YOU JUST READ?

If you enjoyed this book, *please* review it on Amazon and GoodReads!

It's the best way to support the author!

For fantastic fiction, in-depth articles by your favourite authors, open submissions, and more, please...

VISIT OUR WEBSITE
18thwall.com/

LIKE US ON FACEBOOK
facebook.com/18thwall/

FOLLOW US ON TWITTER
@18thWall

We'd love to hear from you!
You help make these books possible.

CASEFILES OF
THE ROYAL OCCULTIST
VOLUME ONE

MONMOUTH'S GIANTS

Josh
Reynolds

The Unwrapping Party

A Complete Short Story from
Casefiles of the Royal Occultist

The beast was dead, to start with. It was a good
way to start the day, to Charles St. Cyprian's
way of thinking. Something hungry and foul had
dredged itself out of the muddy bottom of
Windermere in Cumbria, and it had taken a
week and a day to give it a seeing to, lest it
nibble on the day-trippers. Now, the black
Crossley 20/25 prowled down the Thames
Embankment in the morning fog, Cumbrian mud
crusted on its tires and hood, the driver's fingers
tapping on the wheel. The car was the same
make and model used by the Flying Squad of the
London Metropolitan Police, a fact which its
owner found amusing.

After all, the Royal Occultist was a
policeman of a sort, at least in the Year of Our
Lord 1919. Formed during the reign of Elizabeth
the First, the office of Royal Occultist (or the
Queen's Conjurer, as it had then been known)
had started with the diligent amateur Dr. John
Dee, and passed through a succession of capable
(or not-so capable) hands since. The list was a
long one, weaving in and out of the margins of
British history, and culminating, for the moment,
in one Charles St. Cyprian and his assistant-
cum-apprentice, Ebe Gallowglass.

He looked over at the latter, smiling slightly.
Slender and dark, she was quite obviously 'not

from around here' wherever she went this side of the Nile. Born in a Cairo slum to the unpleasant former priestess of an equally unpleasant cult and a deranged Gaelic occultist, Gallowglass had her mother's looks and her father's temper. She dressed like a man and fought like, well, a woman, which meant she was deadlier than St. Cyprian was entirely comfortable with at times. While shooting things was a large part of the Royal Occultist's job, there were times when decidedly *not* shooting things was the order of the day. If she lived long enough, she'd have his job, and be welcome to it; the 'job' being the investigation, organization and occasional suppression of That Which Man Was Not Meant to Know.

Vampires, ghosts, werewolves, ogres, goblins, hobgoblins, bogles, barguests, boojums and other assorted unclassifiable entities were the purview of the Royal Occultist, as were sorcerers, both foreign and domestic, and the occasional dragon. In short, if it needed to die and the usual methods wouldn't cut it, the Queen's (or King's) Conjurer was on the case.

The title and its offices, such as they were, were bestowed either by the King or Queen, depending upon the gender of the fundament upon the throne, and could only be removed by the same, though Cromwell, bless his black heart, had given it a go. But even the Puritans had had their Witchfinder General in Matthew Hopkins. A horse of another color, but a horse all the same. The holders of the office had ranged from the heroic to the villainous, with a number of stops at marginal and ineffective along the way. St. Cyprian knew that only time would tell how he'd be remembered.

"Brief, but embarrassing, in all likelihood," he muttered, pulling the car up along the sidewalk.

"What is?" Gallowglass said, yawning. She stretched, nearly causing him to ride up onto the pavement. Batting her arm out of the way, he stopped the car.

"Nothing," he said, looking at her. "Have a nice nap, did we?"

"Until you started muttering, yes," she said, rubbing her eyes with a knuckle. "Where are we?"

"Home," St. Cyprian said, getting out. The house at 427 Cheyne Walk was a perk of the job and had been since the Regency. Placed perfectly to watch over certain old structures long hidden by the Thames, the house was unassuming, given its surroundings. Some Royal Occultists had employed staff, but St. Cyprian had never been comfortable with batmen, butlers or the like. Besides which, he had an apprentice to take care of the menial tasks.

"Start the tea, would you?" he said, opening the door and stepping aside to allow Gallowglass to enter ahead of him.

"Coffee," she grunted as she trudged down the hall towards the kitchen, running her hands through the sharp-edged bangs of her hair. "Coffee, then tea," she continued, her voice a dolorous moan.

"As long as it's hot," St. Cyprian said

cheerfully. He had played the part of dogsbody for Thomas Carnacki before the War, even as Carnacki had done for Edwin Drood and Drood had done for Aylmer Beamish and so on and so forth. While it took a Royal decree to make it official, the Royal Occultists had been given tacit permission to pick their own successors after the Restoration. It made things easier all around, and insured, theoretically at least, that the title-bearers were of an appropriate level of competency.

"Or have a replacement waiting, if nothing else," he said out loud, walking into his sitting room, his hands in his pockets. Pictures of former bearers of the office lined the walls, jostling for space with fetish masks and lurid artworks by Goya, Blake and Pickman. Great bookshelves, smelling of British oak and Puritan fires, groaned beneath a library of occult works. Said library was smaller than it should have been, by about three centuries.

"Ta for that, Mr. Cromwell," St. Cyprian said, pulling an unpleasantly large and sharp tooth out of his pocket and grabbing a small chest off one of the bookshelves. The chest was old and ornate, with brass clasps and hinges. Ancient scorch marks marred the treated wood. The Gothic characters inscribed on the lock harkened back to its original owner, Prince Rupert of the Rhine.

Rupert, nephew of Charles the First, had been as energetic a Royal Occultist as he was a cavalry commander, and had spent his short term collecting and organizing the diverse libraries of the former office holders in between crafting treaties with Faerie and driving back incursions from Those Below. Books by Dee, Strange and Subtle, lost Pnakotic texts and hairy bibles of horrid knowledge had all been combined into one of the greatest sources of occult knowledge short of the Papal Libraries. And when Charles had gotten the chop, Cromwell's men had burned Rupert's home and the library with it.

Some of what had been lost had been replaced. Most, though, was gone. Granted, Royal Occultists past had never been meticulous diarists. Except for Drood, who'd paid a number of penny-a-word men to scribble his accomplishments for future generations, at least when they weren't turning said accomplishments into plays and pulps and writing Drood out of his own story. "Bah humbug," St. Cyprian said, popping open the chest and dropping the overlarge fang within.

"Christmas is months away yet," Gallowglass said, from behind him. As he turned, she shoved a steaming mug at him and he was forced to juggle the chest and the coffee for several unpleasant seconds. Glaring at her, he took a gulp and coughed.

"That's not coffee," he said, making a face. "I thought rationing was over."

"It's the best I could scrounge up. We haven't exactly had time for a shop, what with Windermere and that thing with the thing in Dover," Gallowglass said, sipping her own coffee. She blinked and looked at the cup. "I

101

didn't know it could go bad."

"I don't think it was ever good." St. Cyprian set his cup aside and pushed the chest into her arms, deftly snagging her cup before she dropped it. "Put that back, please."

Gallowglass held up the chest and shook it slightly. "When do I get to see what's in this?"

"When you have achieved the seventh level of enlightenment," St. Cyprian said, folding his hands together piously. Gallowglass stuck her tongue out and put the chest back in its spot on the bookshelf. St. Cyprian watched her and his hand idly scratched at his shoulder. There was still a mark there, a physical reminder of their first meeting, a year earlier. It had been less than friendly, as first impressions went. He took a seat and leaned back, sighing in relief. Being yanked beneath the water by a huge slithery thing was exhausting on several levels.

Gallowglass sat opposite him and stretched out in an undignified manner, her muddy boots thumping on the carpet. "What level am I on now, three or four?"

"Too low to calculate accurately," St. Cyprian said.

The doorbell buzzed. The two looked at each other. "I just sat down," Gallowglass said.

"Yes, bully for you. However, you are also my apprentice," St. Cyprian said and he raised a finger in a chiding gesture. "And apprentices get the door."

"I'm your assistant," Gallowglass said.

"It could be ex-assistant," St. Cyprian replied. He closed his eyes and interlaced his fingers over his stomach. The doorbell buzzed again. They maintained a stubborn silence until the third buzz, when Gallowglass threw up her hands with a disgusted sigh and stomped towards the door. She returned a moment later with a card, which she flicked onto St. Cyprian's chest.

St. Cyprian looked at it through narrowed eyes. It was a business card, embossed and covered with the curved shapes of Egyptian hieroglyphics. "What's this?"

"What does it look like?"

"Something annoying," he said. The card would have seemed so much gibberish to anyone not versed in the formal writing system of ancient Egypt. "Who delivered it?"

"Some posh bloke with a face like a man who eats lemons," she said and sniffed. "Dressed like a valet, smelled like a distillery."

"Curiouser and curiouser," St. Cyprian said and picked the card up gingerly. "It's an invitation, apparently."

"Funny looking invitation," Gallowglass said, leaning over the back of his chair. "Who is it from?"

"The Esoteric Order of Thoth-Ra," St. Cyprian said.

Gallowglass snorted.

St. Cyprian glanced at her. "They're not half as silly as they sound. I know every secret society and occult club in London. We're practically drowning in seekers into ancient mysteries and in less than a year, the Esoteric Order of Thoth-Ra has plucked the pearls from

103

the pigs' ears, so to speak. Every half-wit toff with too much money and too much interest in the spooky set has been invited to join. They've poached members from the Mausoleum Club, the Bell Club, the Drones…"

"So they're not fussy," Gallowglass said, sitting down across from him. She glanced aside at the large fireplace, staring hard at the strange faces carved in the mantle. "Neither was Crowley's bunch'."

"Crowley needed funds. Edward Bellingham, from what I gather, does not." St. Cyprian tilted his head back and scrubbed his palms across his face.

Gallowglass smirked.

"You've been playing detective, then, and without me? For shame, Mr. St. Cyprian," she said.

"Perish the thought, Ms. Gallowglass," St. Cyprian said, still looking at the ceiling. "No, I've merely kept my ear to the ground. I—"

A soft snore interrupted him. He looked down, frowning. Gallowglass was curled up in the chair, her eyes closed and her mouth slightly open. St. Cyprian smiled and pushed himself to his feet. He stripped off his coat and draped it over her gently.

He forgot, sometimes, that she was a few years his junior. It was more evident at times like these, when she relaxed into something approaching softness and the hard edge of her experience drifted away. Both of them had been ill-used by life, and would likely continue to be so. Their line of work wasn't a long one or a straight one. He looked up at the pictures. Painted eyes, sorrowful, arrogant, fearful and mad, looked down on them and for a moment, he felt the weight of ages on his soul.

Some Royal Occultists retired, but most died. By accident or by design, they died and were replaced by royal edict, like stripped out cogs plucked from a machine, lest they damage the mechanism. Carnacki had been one such cog. His eyes found the oil-on-canvas ones of his mentor and friend. He stood in front of the painting, looking up at it, his hands clasped behind his back.

St. Cyprian remembered that first night he'd spent listening to Carnacki's stories in this very room, with Dodgson and Arkwright and the others. Just before Franz Ferdinand had taken an assassin's bullet to the brainpan and touched off a Continental firestorm. He closed his eyes, old aches springing again to prominence, and he felt the trails of old scars beneath his clothes.

The scars, earned at Ypres in the closing year of the War, traced his evolution from a callow youth to a slightly-less callow man. It had been a quick one as such things went; two bullets deep and one long. His thigh ached abominably in the damp, but he was learning to live with the phantom physical pain, if not the spiritual. Carnacki had died at Ypres, blown out of one life and into the next. One moment he'd been there, and the next…

St. Cyprian looked away and his hands clenched so tightly that his knuckles popped. Absently, he stuffed a hand in his pocket. His fingers found the card. He withdrew it and looked at the hieroglyphs. It was a fancy way of playing mysterious. He frowned again, rubbing his thumb across the embossed figures.

What he knew of Edward Bellingham, the self-proclaimed Grand Vizier of the Esoteric Order of Thoth-Ra, read like a patch out of Strachey's *Eminent Victorians*. Bellingham had been at Old College, Oxford for a brief period in the early days of the century before being sent packing under a dark cloud. Something to do with Egyptian antiquities was the rumor. Bellingham had trundled off to the Sudan before vanishing entirely for the duration of the War.

Then, in 1918, he'd come back. He had money and could mumbo with the best of the jumbos and had subsequently founded the EOTR for the high-stockings. In truth, most occult groups were nothing but harmless would-be pilgrims. Even Crowley's lot, despite their growling, were little more than dilettantes. Crowley himself was another story, but he was safely in United States, which meant he was someone else's problem. But Bellingham…there was something there.

He'd received regular invitations to attend the meetings of the Esoteric Order of Thoth-Ra since it had opened its doors. So far, he'd refused. The Royal Occultist couldn't be seen to favor one faction over another. While most of the bookhounds of Olde London Towne were harmless sorts, others were dangerous, especially in groups.

St. Cyprian chewed his lip. In the War, he'd

106

been able to *feel* an artillery barrage before it hit. Like hearing thunder in your bones, or feeling rain in your joints. He had that same feeling now, closing in from all sides. There was a storm gathering, and they needed to be at its eye.

St. Cyprian eyed the card, as if hoping it would reveal Bellingham's secrets. Nothing was forthcoming, however. He sighed and slipped it back into his pocket and then went to make himself some tea.

When evening came and they had rested, bathed and eaten St. Cyprian felt more human than he had in days. Bundling Gallowglass into the Crossley took less effort than he'd feared. Normally, such occult-orientated gatherings held little interest for his assistant, a fact which he blamed on the oddities of her upbringing. Mostly, he was content to leave her be, but tonight he couldn't help but fear he was going to need her. Luckily, Gallowglass didn't require any convincing.

"Of course I want to go to the—what'd you call it?" she said.

"It's an unwrapping party, apparently, mummies and that sort of rot. A bit passé as the modern set judge things, but among the psychical crowd it's still a done thing," St. Cyprian said and fiddled with his tie. His suit was Savile Row, straight from Gieves & Hawkes. "Mostly cats, though."

"Cats," Gallowglass said darkly.

"Cats," St. Cyprian said, nodding. "Barmy for cats, your ancient Egyptian. Whole temples devoted to Ulthar's own, what? Dozens of the

107

poor pusses are found every year, wrapped tighter than a footballer's ankle after a scrum and there's nothing your basic Theosophist likes better than unwrap 'em, preferably over wine and cheeses while singing hymns to Bast."

"I hate cats," Gallowglass said, shuddering. She didn't elaborate, and St. Cyprian knew better than to pry. Gallowglass had grown up in the slums of Cairo, and though the pharaohs were long dust, the gods they had worshipped still had some power in that land, despite the best efforts of Turk and Englishman alike.

"I don't think this is a cat," he said, gesturing with the invitation as they left the flat. The Crossley sat on the street, where they'd left it. "Bellingham wouldn't bother sending me an invitation to see some curried stray being skinned of its linen vestments, I don't think. No, he's got something large in mind."

"Good," Gallowglass said, hunching forward, "Because I bloody hate cats."

"So you said."

"Just reiterating for future reference," she said, glaring around her, as if to remind the world of its place. She shivered and slid into the Crossley. St. Cyprian got behind the wheel and within a few minutes, they were off, heading towards Seven Dials.

Barely more than two decades prior, Seven Dials had been more popularly known as St. Giles Rookery, and had been one of the worst slums that London had to offer. The area had become a byword for squalor and depravity, and had hosted more than its fair share of occult-types—palm readers, clairvoyants, herbalists and the like had occupied, and indeed, likely still did occupy, the crooked lanes and hidden storefronts of the area. There were also Bolsheviks, Anarchists and Mafioso crowding each other in the garrets, taverns and side-streets. Too, more than one esoteric society had settled roots into the coiling streets, including Theosophists, Freemasons and the ever-present Swedenborgians. And, of course, the Esoteric Order of Thoth-Ra.

On the whole, Seven Dials was a tangy sort of stew, and one St. Cyprian rarely visited, unless it was in a professional capacity. Previous incumbents had tried, more than once, to drive the money-changers out of the temple, so to speak, but St. Cyprian had lived through a mundane war and found he had no taste for the occult variety; he acted only when necessary. It was bad enough dealing with foreigners whose knowledge of the invisible far out-stripped his own; going up against the Sisterhood of Rats or the Si-Fan when, by and large, they adequately policed themselves, was not something he looked forward to. If some bunch of amateur, fifth form demonologists wanted to summon Mephistopheles without considering the consequences that was their business. But sometimes...sometimes it spilled over. And that was where the Royal Occultist came in.

The orange sky of early evening had slid into the purple of twilight when they finally reached the house that had been claimed as the ritual center of the EOTR. Around them, Seven Dials

109

woke up for the evening. Bawdy laughter sounded from the open windows of nearby garrets, and cars honked and chugged through the streets.

"Are you sure this is the place?" Gallowglass said, tilting her head to peer up at the house.

St. Cyprian stepped out of the Crossley. "Quite," he said, as Gallowglass joined him. He glanced at her and raised an eyebrow. "Is that my suit?"

"You only just noticed?" She grinned and snapped the braces holding up her trousers. She wore a man's suit with the trouser and sleeve cuffs rolled up to accommodate the difference in height, and an eight-panel cap akin to the sort newsboys wore. "We might need to run." Patting the lapel of her borrowed suit coat, she said, "And I thought it might be a good idea to hide the lemon squeezer." She twitched the edge of the coat aside and St. Cyprian saw the holstered shape of a revolver.

"I don't recall asking you to bring a pistol," he said.

"You never have to ask," she said, shoving her hands in her trouser pockets and slumping against the Crossley. "Besides, we're walking into a den of iniquity. I might need to shoot a lock off or a light out or something of the sort."

St. Cyprian looked at the house, which was indistinguishable from any other low-rent house in Seven Dials, and snorted. "Oh yes. Practically satanic, that house."

"Hiding in plain sight, the bastards." Gallowglass shoved the brim of her cap up.

"Let's go see if we have the right place then, shall we?" he said, striding towards the house. As he drew close to the door, he saw that there was one difference between it and the others that surrounded it. On the door, just above the knocker, a strange, recursive symbol had been carved into the wood. It was eerily familiar, and St. Cyprian felt a chill as he tried to grasp its shape. Reaching out, he rapped on the door, his rings adding a sharp edge to the sound. The three steel rings were, like the house on Cheyne Walk, part and parcel of the office, though St. Cyprian still had little idea of what they were for, if anything. Carnacki had insisted on wearing them, and St. Cyprian saw little reason not to do the same.

The door swung open and a blast of music washed over them. A man wearing the uniform of a butler and a highly-stylized Egyptian death-mask stepped into view. The butler nodded diffidently and extended a gloved hand. "Your card, sir," he said, his voice echoing strangely from within the confines of the mask.

St. Cyprian extended the card, his eyes narrowed. "I wasn't aware that this was a costume party," he said.

"Ceremonial dress, sir," the butler said tonelessly. He accepted the card, flipped it over several times, and then stepped aside. "Please enter, Mr. St. Cyprian, you and your guest."

At the other end of the corridor, a set of double doors painted in the fashion of an Egyptian temple were pulled open to admit them. The music rose in volume and they stepped into a large room, crowded with figures and furniture alike. More servants, all in masks similar to the butler's, threaded through the crowd with practiced grace, bearing trays and bottles. The music was distinctly foreign, full of the buzzing rhythms of the Arabian Peninsula. Lit braziers decorated the corners, expelling sweetly scented smoke.

Gallowglass took a sniff. "Smells like home."

"As well it should. The smell and the sound of the thing are the surest pathways to the soul of the thing, as they say," someone said. St. Cyprian and Gallowglass turned. A heavy-set man stood behind them, a silk robe thrown over his wool suit and a fez perched on his bulbous head. He placed his hands together and bowed shallowly. "Mr. St. Cyprian, your presence here adds to our web of light. I'm glad you finally decided to attend one of my soirees."

St. Cyprian inclined his head. "Edward Bellingham, I presume," he said.

"None other," Bellingham said. He smiled thinly. "Might I say, sir, that I am an avowed—ah—fan of your work?" He waved a hand to indicate their surroundings. "I am sure that my humble temple of mysteries isn't a patch on what you're used to."

St. Cyprian spared the room a glance. It wasn't humble in the slightest, Bellingham's protestations to the contrary. Expensive tapestries, likely Moorish in origin, hung from walls which were decorated with Egyptian hieroglyphs and Etruscan bas-reliefs. It was a garish nightmare of conflicting cultures, all exploited for their exoticism to English eyes.

When he turned his attentions back to Bellingham, he noted that the man was watching him closely, his dark eyes amused. "A bit patchwork, you might say," Bellingham said.

"By design," St. Cyprian said. It wasn't a question. Bellingham inclined his head.

"Egypt grows more familiar to the jaded eyes of our fair metropolis by the day," Bellingham said. "Dedicated orientalists scour the world, ferreting out secrets." He made a loose gesture. "I simply strive to inject some mystery back into things."

"And extract a bit of dosh in the process?" St. Cyprian said.

Bellingham's smile turned frosty. "A man has a right to make a living. The Esoteric Order of Thoth-Ra is open to all men." He glanced at Gallowglass. "And women too, of course."

"Cheers," Gallowglass said, snagging a glass off a passing tray.

Bellingham chuckled. "I'm glad you came, sir, for tonight is a very special night indeed!"

"Oh?"

"Quite so, quite so! One of our most esteemed members has even now returned from the Valley of the Kings with a prize worthy of...well...a king!" Bellingham's smile threatened to spill past the confines of his cheeks.

"And what's that then?" St. Cyprian said, his eyes narrowing.

Bellingham tapped the side of his nose.

"Wait and see, sir, wait and see." With that, he gave another of peculiar bows and then spun and bounded off, like an excited school-boy. Gallowglass watched him go and knocked back her champagne.

"Rum sort," she said.

"The rummiest," St. Cyprian agreed. He looked at the crowd. There were some familiar faces there, men and women whom he'd had contact with at one time or another. In the corner, beneath the gaze of a stone bust of the great god Pan, Dion Fortune—formerly Violet Mary Firth—was arguing in increasingly loud tones with several other members of the Hermetic Order of the Golden Dawn. St. Cyprian wondered whether she was one of Bellingham's newest recruits; by all accounts, Fortune wasn't happy with the Order and they certainly weren't happy with her. They'd kicked Crowley to the curb as well, he recalled.

Near the buffet the young vintner and would-be author Dennis Wheatley was chatting amiably with the writer, Elliott O'Donnell, as well as Rollo Ahmed, who was a fraud, albeit a friendly one. Ahmed, who claimed to be Egyptian but was, according to most of St. Cyprian's sources, actually from Guyana, raised a hand in a gesture of greeting as he caught sight of St. Cyprian. St. Cyprian smiled and returned the greeting. "Before us ebbs and flows a veritable sea of sins and infractions, Ms. Gallowglass. It's a who's who of the sorcerous set."

"Den of iniquity, innit," she said, sniffing.

114

"Glad I brought the pistol now?"

St. Cyprian didn't reply. He made his way into the crowd, Gallowglass at his heels.

"What's the plan?" she said.

"We mingle."

"Mingle? That a code for something?" she said.

"Yes, it's code for mingling," he said, glancing at her. "Try not to embarrass me."

"I can hob with the best of the nobs, no fear," Gallowglass said. "We aren't here for drinks and caviar, are we?"

"No," St. Cyprian said. "Or, at least not entirely; we're here for the show." He gestured, indicating a bandstand that had been set up along the far wall. Heavy braziers had been mounted at the corners, and a wine-red curtain had been tacked to the wall. The curtain bore the same symbol as had been on the front door, albeit larger and splayed across its folds. "Keep your eyes and ears open. Mingle."

"Mingling," she said, giving a two-fingered salute. She snagged another champagne glass as she disappeared into the crowd. St. Cyprian turned back to the stage. He sidled closer, his hands in his pockets.

A large circle had been painted on the stage, its radius extending to each corner. He sniffed and recognized the smell of certain strange unguents; it was a familiar mixture. His predecessor Carnacki had showed him how to mix it, from a recipe recorded in the Sigsand Manuscript. It was a protective circle; a pentacle, in actuality…evil forces couldn't enter it, or, in the event they were inside, couldn't leave it. "Now why would he need that?" he murmured.

Something was off about the whole evening, he thought. He looked around the room and his senses, both physical and otherwise, reached out. There was a pall over everything and he was put in mind of what a hare must feel, as the fox closes in. Something was coming, something vast and terrible and he had no idea where it was coming from or what form it would take, and that made him very nervous indeed.

He was tempted to find Gallowglass and leave. Let the play-actors deal with the consequences of their actions. But he knew that if he did, it would be worse than just a few dead amateurs. As he pondered, Bellingham climbed up on the stage and clapped his hands for silence. It fell in swathes, as the crowd realized that something was happening.

"Ladies and gentlemen," Bellingham said, his voice carrying easily. He held up his hands, his oversize sleeves dropping down to his elbows, exposing his surprisingly brawny forearms. Tarnished bracers that had the look of something pried from an Egyptian tomb decorated his arms. "I am so glad that so many of you could be here tonight!" Bellingham went on. "For a year, we have undertaken an exploration of the Great Mysteries of the East together; we have plumbed the unutterable depths and scaled the remotest heights..." Bellingham gestured for emphasis.

He was theatrical, but then, all the best

conmen were. St. Cyprian listened with one ear while he surreptitiously scanned the crowd. Where was Gallowglass?

"But tonight…ah, tonight, we shall all partake of incandescent ambrosia, my friends, as I have promised!" Bellingham said floridly. He flung out a hand. "Come forth, Brother Parker!" he shouted, and the crowd at last fell completely silent.

Heads turned as wheels squeaked. Masked attendants wheeled in a large gurney with a long, covered shape on it. A thin, nervous looking man trotted beside it, his face pale and strained. The hairs on the back of St. Cyprian's neck prickled as he watched the attendants move their burden to the stage. Someone had turned off the music. Everything was quiet, save for the squeak of the gurney wheels.

"Brother Parker, returned from the dim avenues of the Valley of the Kings, with the very prize I promised you all at the beginning of this communal journey to Khem's black shores," Bellingham said, spreading him arms. "Bring it up, gentlemen! Bring it up, lest we waste the night in awestruck wonder!"

The attendants hefted their burden, gurney and all, and carried it up onto the stage. They deposited it dead-center in the pentacle, and St. Cyprian blinked. The old artillery feeling was back now, and strong. He could practically hear the whistle of incoming shells. What was on that gurney?

Bellingham gestured, and someone dimmed the lights, leaving the only illumination the

117

flickering glow from the braziers. "It is said, by the wise men of the American Indians, that wisdom sits in places," Bellingham said, folding his hands together. "That certain spots soak up the very stuff of history. The Valley of the Kings could be said to be such a place, I'd wager. It houses the sleeping souls of history's greatest monarchs, including a few whose names are unknown save to jackals..." Bellingham snapped his fingers.

One of the attendants whipped the covering off, revealing what lay on the gurney. The crowd gasped appropriately as the sarcophagus was revealed. Bellingham leaned over it, his fingers creeping over its bare surface. "You see it before you, fellow knowledge-seekers. The sarcophagus of one of the greatest men ever forgotten by history. The last pharaoh of the Third Dynasty, whose name was stricken from the holy writ..."

St. Cyprian found himself leaning forward. Attendants gripped the feet and head of the sarcophagus. Parker stepped back, his hand twitching towards his coat. St. Cyprian frowned as Bellingham snapped out a hand to drop a grip on the other man's wrist, holding him in place. With his free hand, he gestured upwards, and the attendants carefully levered the sarcophagus open. He could see that the seals had already been broken, likely in preparation for this big reveal.

"Behold, he who was known as the Doom of All Mankind! Behold, the Black Pharaoh! Behold...NEPHREN-KA!"

A cloud of dust rose from the opened sarcophagus, obscuring St. Cyprian's view of Bellingham for a moment. The name of the sarcophagus' occupant rang through his mind like the rumble of distant guns or thunder playing among black clouds. It couldn't be, could it? But the rush of sheer, black malevolence that swept over him as the syllables of the name settled on his mind like a gargoyle-weight told him otherwise.

This was Nephren-Ka, the Black Pharaoh, one of only a handful of pharaohs ever erased from the peculiar bureaucratic records of the Egyptian dynasties, his name hidden even as those of Akhenaten and Nitocris were. The reasons were lost, but they had likely been damn good ones.

The dust cleared and for a moment, Bellingham's eyes met his own. A chill caressed St. Cyprian's spine. The gleam of triumph in Bellingham's eyes was unmistakable.

"Oh hell," he muttered, looking around for Gallowglass.

Bellingham waved aside the dust and gave a loud chuckle. "Yes, my friends, yes, this is the last earthly remains of him whom a centuries' worth of mystics have sought! And thanks to the dedication of Brother Parker, we have found him!"

As the crowd made appropriate noises, St. Cyprian felt something building beneath his feet. His hair stiffened, like a dog's hackles, and he felt strange electricity prickling along the edges of his consciousness. Something was happening.

119

Something…

The groan, when it came, was so deep as to be almost mistaken for the distant rumble of the District Line passing through Earls Court. It stretched out, reaching every corner of the makeshift temple and bringing everyone inside to abrupt, horrified attention. It was a sound full of weight and pain and color drained from every face in the crowd. Bellingham swallowed, the triumphant glee gone from his face, replaced by consternation.

"Yes…yes, you hear him?" he said, speaking over the deep, dull sound, though with difficulty. "Even in death, his *ka* clings to his body, held by chains of secrets that no man remembers, save me." Bellingham looked at his audience, holding them in silence by sheer force of will. It was impressive, St. Cyprian had to admit.

"But the dead are no threat to the living, not even dead sorcerer kings," Bellingham went on. He motioned to the stage. "Though a bit of preparation doesn't hurt." The crowd tittered appreciatively, but fell silent as the groan rose in volume. It was an almost spiteful sound, like the growl of a tiger in a cage. The sarcophagus shuddered slightly, causing the gurney to rattle. Bellingham licked his lips and stepped back and snapped his fingers.

"It is said, in the Sudan, that unlucky is the town whose wizards are not yet ashes," he said. "There is some truth in that, my friends. For the power of a sorcerer, like a fine wine, only grows stronger as it sits contained. It ferments as the worms grow fat. Nephren-Ka was the equal to the sorcerer kings of the lost antediluvian kingdoms named in the Chaldean Fragments or the Cimmerian Scrolls; imagine, my fellow pilgrims, what rare brew then sits before us in this humble sarcophagus!"

The groan rose in pitch, spiraling up into an angry shriek. Glasses trembled in people's hands, vibrating sympathetically to the sound. St. Cyprian winced. The necessity of the protective circle was plain now. Whatever was in that sarcophagus, ancient pharaoh or otherwise, wasn't happy about the current situation. The braziers flared, spitting embers and smoke. People drew back from the stage. Bellingham raised his hands, calling for calm.

"Pay no heed to his snarls," Bellingham said. His face was damp with sweat. "Nephren-Ka is dead and his ability to wreak harm is dead with him! But his power remains still and as I have promised, it will be ours!"

St. Cyprian realized suddenly what was going on. This was no mere unwrapping party. It was something much, much worse.

"We shall feast upon the very essence of power itself!" Bellingham shouted. With a flourish, he pulled a curvy bladed *kris* knife from within his robes. "We shall do as the ancients did and taste of the flesh of the sorcerer and become as him!"

"Damnation," St. Cyprian said, hands clenching. "Bellingham, you stupid fool!"

"Oi," Gallowglass hissed urgently, squirming through the crowd towards him. "I think we've got trouble!" She had one hand in her coat,

121

ready to draw her pistol.

"Really, do tell," St. Cyprian snapped, his eyes still on the stage.

"Doors are locked. Bellingham doesn't want anybody leaving, and his fancy boys are armed to the pants," Gallowglass muttered.

The flames in the braziers turned blue. There was a foul stink on the air, like ancient damp rising through old stones and it was growing stronger by the minute.

"By their smell shall ye know them," he muttered.

"Smells like the gas has sprung a leak," Gallowglass said.

The gurney was trembling now and visibly. The braziers wobbled on their iron legs. Bellingham was calling for silence as the crowd began to shift and roil. Panic was in the air.

"Nothing for it," St. Cyprian said out loud, moving towards the stage. If Bellingham saw him coming, he gave no sign. The pudgy magus was too busy trying to calm his audience.

"What are you doing?" Gallowglass called after him.

"Getting in on the act," St. Cyprian said. He needed to stop Bellingham before the man did the unthinkable. He pushed towards the stage. He could feel the floorboards bending and breathing beneath the thick carpet. No one was listening to Bellingham. People were beginning to turn towards the doors, primitive survival instincts prompting the herd towards safety. Only those doors were locked, and none of Bellingham's masked attendants were giving ground.

"Friends, why do you rush to leave?" Bellingham bellowed. "Would you forsake greatness? We are all bound to this journey by bonds of aetheric harmony, are we not? Friends! Friends!"

He reached the stage and began to run up the stairs. Gallowglass had been right; he should have brought a weapon. On his hand, the three rings began to grow unpleasantly warm. "Stop right there," a high-pitched voice said. St. Cyprian froze, his foot on the top step of the stage.

"Whoop," he said, looking up into the barrel of a Mauser, clutched in Brother Parker's sweaty hand.

"Who are you? What are you doing?" Parker nearly shrieked. His eyes were wide and showing too much white and St. Cyprian knew that Brother Parker had gone quietly, savagely mad somewhere between Cairo and Seven Dials. What had he heard, trapped aboard a cramped steamer with the thing in its box? What had it whispered to him as it groaned and scratched? "Bellingham!"

"Parker, what are you doing?" Bellingham snarled, turning. His eyes widened slightly as he took in the tableau and then they narrowed in anger. "You…are you responsible for this?" he said, glaring at St. Cyprian. "I should have known! I invited you here to show you that I did not fear you, that your antiquated notions of magic and sorcery held no power over me, but you couldn't have that, could you? What have you done?"

St. Cyprian stepped up onto the stage, hands raised as Parker stepped back. He stood relaxed, ignoring the trembling barrel of the Mauser that lingered perilously close to his head. He reached slowly into his coat and pulled out his silver cigarette case. Taking one out, he made a show of tapping it on the side of the case before placing it between his lips. "Nothing, but then, I'm sure you're well aware of that, Mr. Bellingham."

"He's lying!" Parker said. His face was gray from fear. "He's come to free it! He'll set it on us, the damned monster!"

"Shut *up* Parker," Bellingham barked. The braziers were moving as if being swung around and around. Smoke and embers scattered across the stage. The tapestries on the walls were rippling as if rats crawled behind them. There were long shadows on the walls and ceiling, stretching like the talons of some immense beast.

"The circle—the markings—they aren't enough, Bellingham," St. Cyprian said carefully. The smoke circles floated around his head. He'd learned the art of blowing protective circles from an Ostyak shaman in Siberia, though he doubted it would do much good against whatever was pressing against the Outside even now. He could feel something, like the buzzing of scarab beetles, in his head. A humming, whispering voice beneath the bestial groaning.

"Quiet!" Bellingham said, licking his lips. "They should have been enough. The books said

124

they would be!"

"Books can be wrong," St. Cyprian said, stepping forward. "We have to close it! Get the top back on it and reseal it! That might stop it, or put it back to sleep."

"Stay away from it," Parker snarled, his Mauser twitching. "Don't let him get near it!"

"Silence, Parker!" Bellingham growled, but St. Cyprian knew he'd lost whatever hold he'd had on the other man. He saw the thread of sanity give way and then the Mauser rose like a cobra's snout.

"No! I won't let him do it—not to me! I won't let it get me!"

The pistol gave a short, sharp sound and St. Cyprian felt a bullet tug at his coat. He dove across the distance between them, driving his fist up into Parker's belly. The air went out of the smaller man in a whoosh and he folded over St. Cyprian's arm.

He let Parker fall and snatched up the Mauser, spinning around in time to see Bellingham sinking to his knees, his face white with shock as he clutched at his bloody arm. Evidently his coat hadn't been the only thing to feel the bite of Parker's shot.

"Damn it," he said, hurrying towards the fallen magus. He wasn't so much concerned with Bellingham's health as he was with the consequences of spilling blood inside a magical circle. He'd seen the results of that more than once, and it was never pleasant. "Get up Bellingham! Get out of the circle!"

"He—he shot me!" Bellingham blubbered.

Shots rang out, plucking at the stage. St. Cyprian skidded to a halt as several of the death-masked servants shoved their way through the crowd towards the stage. One he recognized as the doorman barked an order and pointed at St. Cyprian. They'd seen the gun in his hand and made assumptions, obviously. Gallowglass had hers out as well, and she overturned a table as the servants swung their weapons towards her. Bullets cracked and the crowd gave a communal scream and the doors bucked on their hinges as somebody went at them with a credenza.

The stage squirmed beneath his feet. He heard again the cracking of wood and he felt as if he were stepping on a bed of snakes. A bullet spoke loud near his ear and without thinking he returned fire, old instincts rising to the fore. The Mauser bucked in his hand and there was a scream, but he didn't stop to see if he'd actually hit anyone. He stooped, reaching for Bellingham's arm.

The magus looked up at him blearily, his fez askew. "What?"

"Up, man. Get up!" St. Cyprian snapped. A brazier toppled over, spilling coals and fire across the stage. It seemed as if the whole room was shaking. St. Cyprian jerked Bellingham up even as he realized that the strange groaning that had punctuated the beginning of Bellingham's aborted ritual had ceased. All was silent, save for the crackle of flames.

The hairs on the back of his neck prickled and he turned, still gripping Bellingham. The thing in the sarcophagus had sat up. Brown, leathery flesh rubbed against ancient bone as the narrow, almost vulpine head turned towards him. Eyes like those of a beast just beyond the light of a campfire met his own and he felt his blood turn to ice in his veins.

Nephren-Ka was awake.

It was a thin thing, in the way of all the mummified dead; drained and dried to brittle slenderness. Yet, somehow, this thing still possessed a hideous vitality. The bandages were blackened as if by fire and the skull was somehow *wrong* in its shape and dimensions. The lean jaw opened slowly and St. Cyprian swallowed as dozens of crooked fangs were revealed.

In life, Nephren-Ka had been a man. But in death, he was something else entirely. The mummy's eyes blazed with a malignant awareness that seemed to transcend the physical. As it glared at him, St. Cyprian felt as if his soul were an onion being peeled, layer upon layer. There was a monstrous power in that gaze, and he recalled what Bellingham had said about fermenting sorcerers and wondered what sort of brew Nephren-Ka had become after untold centuries. Only with difficulty did he look away and bring the Mauser to bear. But before he could fire, Bellingham grabbed awkwardly for his arm.

"No! I can't let you destroy it!" the fat man bawled.

"Let go of me, Bellingham!" St. Cyprian said, jerking his hand free. A shadow fell over him. The mummy had risen to its feet in the sarcophagus, dust and strange oils scattered everywhere by its too-fluid movements. He brought the Mauser up and fired. The dead thing staggered but did not fall. With a hiss that was half way between that of a snake and man, it sprang towards him, eyes blazing horribly. A withered paw snatched the pistol from his grip and crushed it into a shapeless lump with seeming ease. Hands stinging from the force of the blow, St. Cyprian tumbled back, falling over Bellingham. His eyes met those of the mummy, and he felt fish-hooks of pure, terrible power slide into his soul as his third eye sprang open of its own accord.

The spirit-eye, Carnacki had called it. St. Cyprian had learned how to open it from a Tibetan lama of his acquaintance. Aside from having what St. Cyprian considered an unhealthy fascination for the color green, the lama had been a good teacher. Humans were, by and large, as sensitive to the paranormal as animals were to earthquakes. But they put on blinders instinctively, blocking out everything but what was ahead of them. The inability of the human mind to correlate all of its perceptions was one of humanity's built-in defenses against the many, *many* predatory malignancies that swam through the outer void. In the trade, you had to shuck those evolutionary blinders first thing, lest the sharks snap you up all unawares.

But sometimes seeing was just as bad as not seeing. Instinctively, he had opened the eye, and had been exposed to the unfettered horror of his attacker. St. Cyprian screamed as he saw the

128

hunched malevolence that hunkered above Nephren-Ka, the source and cause of his hideous transformation; it was at once a void and horribly, hideously full of writhing, cancerous *shapes*. This was the reason he had been stricken from the litany of kings, this was why his tomb had been placed where even jackals feared to tread.

Nephren-Ka had been touched by something from Outside, and had been changed by it. Where the pharaoh's soul had once been there was now only a coruscating typhoon of cosmic blasphemy.

St. Cyprian thrust out his hands to keep the thing off as Nephren-Ka lunged...and then fell back with a piercing shriek. The mummy staggered in a circle, clawing at its skull. St. Cyprian looked down blankly, mind still reeling from his brief contact with the soul of the Black Pharaoh, and saw that he had fallen out of the protective circle. For the moment, the creature was still trapped. Nephren-Ka turned, its yellow gaze falling on Bellingham, who stared at it in horror, his mouth gaping soundlessly.

Before it could fall on him, however, the gun-toting servants intervened. Whatever grim spell had held them frozen was gone now, dashed aside by the threat to their employer. Pistols spoke eloquent and Nephren-Ka spun and danced awkwardly, its skeletal frame punctured by a dozen hornets of hot lead. Yet still, it did not fall. Almost casually, it stalked towards the edge of the stage and then paused, as if considering. Then, with a contemptuous gesture, it tipped over the gurney and the sarcophagus, obscuring part of the circle.

It hissed again, and this time there was a note of foul triumph in the sound. Nephren-Ka bounded across its makeshift bridge and dove onto the closest of the gunmen, its jaws spreading impossibly wide. The man's scream was cut short as his head was swallowed by the thing. Its blackened teeth snapped together with almost comical precision and the man's head vanished. The headless body fell, blood pumping from the ragged stump of the neck. Nephren-Ka whirled, quicker than thought as gunshots plucked at it. An insect-thin arm snapped out, grabbing a second gunman by his waistcoat and jerking him into the air. The man screamed for help as the mummy dashed him down to the floor. The floorboards snapped and splintered and only the man's twitching hands and feet were visible above the edges of the broken boards.

"Up," Gallowglass said, hooking his arm. She had climbed up on the stage as soon as the mummy had lunged off. Her face was strained and pale, and the pistol trembled in her grip.

"Where's Bellingham?" St. Cyprian said as he got to his feet. He felt wrung out and soul-sick from his brief contact with the thing.

"Scarpered, the great tub of suet," Gallowglass said. "I don't blame him." Heat from the growing flames washed over them. The curtains and tapestries had caught fire now, and the whole place was likely to go up. They had to get out.

Unfortunately, Nephren-Ka was between them and the door. The mummy crouched over a dying man, slowly, inexorably squeezing the life out of him, its fingers dug deep into the flesh of his throat. Blood welled, coating its palms, and it released its hold, letting the body fall. It turned and then shied away from the fire, shaking its head.

St. Cyprian's eyes narrowed, and a sudden, tiny ember of hope surged. Was it afraid of the fire? As if in response to that thought, the fleshless jaws moved. Air escaped, and maybe what might have been words, had there been a tongue and vocal cords and lungs to shape them. Instead, it was just a bone-deep groan. The eyes blazed brighter even than the fires that surrounded it as it trotted towards them.

"Back off," Gallowglass snarled, and her Webley-Fosbery snarled with her. The big revolver chewed chunks out of the loping horror, but as before, it barely slowed. No man-made weapon was going to do the job, not against something like that.

St. Cyprian cast around desperately for something—anything—that could be used as a weapon. Fire, if it was afraid of fire—he had to use fire. But how, it wasn't as if the creature was going to stand still and let him burn it...

He gestured towards the stage. "The circle's still intact! All we have to do is trap the damn thing back in Bellingham's circle and let nature take its course!" He turned towards her. "Miss Gallowglass, get out of here!"

"What about you?" She reloaded and aimed

her useless pistol at the approaching mummy. It was grinning at them with a daemonic eagerness that caused St. Cyprian's soul to quaver. Nephren-Ka was no soulless engine of murder, existing only to rend and slay. No, there was a mind in that cacodemonical shell, a blasted black brain that had howled in silent captivity for dark, unremembered eons. Now that it was free, there was no telling what it would do, should it escape. He saw foul promises in the glittering, lupine eyes of the monster as it approached.

"I'm the bait," he said, shoving her toward the stage stairs.

Nephren-Ka's jaws chattered in what might have been laughter as it sprang onto the stage, the gurney clattering beneath its weight. St. Cyprian scooped up a brazier and swung it, slinging burning embers towards the dark, spidery shape closing in on him. The mummy dodged the embers with boneless ease. A bloody claw stretched towards St. Cyprian's face.

Gallowglass, ignoring his orders, fired her pistol. The mummy spun and shrieked. She backed away, still firing, as it loped towards her. St. Cyprian, cursing, swatted it with the brazier. It whirled, jaws snapping.

"Move," St. Cyprian shouted. Gallowglass leapt off the stage.

Hurling the brazier, he dove under the mummy's lunge and scrambled towards the gurney and sarcophagus. He hit both, knocking them aside and out of the circle. He fell to the floor and scrambled to his feet. The mummy loomed over him, its posture one of frustration.

Without the gurney in the way, the circuit of the circle was whole once more. Nephren-Ka raised its hands and pawed ineffectually at the air. "Oh no chum, you're nicked," St. Cyprian said, with a bravado that he didn't feel. Something burned his neck and he leapt back, looking up. Fire crawled across the ceiling, causing the wallpaper to curl and bubble. "You're going to burn, you bastard," he continued, pointing at the creature. "And I'd say it's far past time for it."

"Come on, enough admiring your handiwork," Gallowglass barked, grabbing his arm.

He turned to follow her. A snarl, like that of a leopard, made him turn back. Nephren-Ka stared at him, its face working stiffly. Fire fell across its shoulders, and it flinched, folding in on itself. Burning paper and cloth floated through the hot air, momentarily obscuring St. Cyprian's vision. The mummy whined deep in its throat and sank down, almost as if it were shrinking. For a moment, he thought it had worked, that the creature was gone.

Then, the stage collapsed, its struts weakened by the fire and the leaping and crashing. St. Cyprian stared in shock as the mummy sprang from the wreckage and leapt through the curtain of fire, sizzling talons stretched out to grab and rend and kill. He only had a moment to shove Gallowglass aside before the creature crashed into him, jaws snapping and claws digging into the soft meat of his throat. It bore him

133

backwards and they fell to the floor, the creature atop him, its fingers around his throat, its fangs snapping wildly at his face as he frantically grabbed its jaw and tried to shove it away.

As they struggled, it's eyes locked with his and he saw images, pieces of other times, memories of a black pyramid, built so that no light could enter it, and what had crawled, bat-winged and burning-eyed out of the cracks in that darkness to murmur sinister wisdoms to the young pharaoh. He saw the revolt of the nobles and heard chariots rattle over the plazas as arrows hissed and men screamed and died as Nephren-Ka's voice reached out from the apex of the black pyramid and dug its claws into every man's soul. He heard Nephren-Ka's screams as he was shut into his box, and spells were woven to keep him trapped forever and a day. He felt the agony of transformation as the Black Pharaoh's body became something else in the darkness and a horrid realization stole over him: Nephren-Ka's transformation was not yet finished.

The creature before him, stinking of charred linen and spoiled meat was but a chrysalis for something larger and infinitely more terrible than any old dead thing. It had taken centuries to reach this stage, and would likely take centuries still for it to reach its final form. Nephren-Ka had bargained away not just his soul, but his humanity as well, and now the devil was taking its due. Strange things moved within the dried, charred form of the mummy, like maggots in a corpse. The creature was a wound in the flesh of the world, and something was squirming through the gap down the long passage of years.

Black tendrils, glistening with wet, poked through the bindings, coiling and twisting blindly and he gagged in disgust as they stretched towards him. Nephren-Ka's eyes blazed and it uttered its croaking laugh again. Then Gallowglass had her arm around the creature's throat, choking its laugh short and the barrel of her Webley was pressed to the side of its head. Her teeth were bared in a snarl of fear and rage as she pulled the trigger until the pistol clicked dry and the thing flung her aside with a scream. She hit the floor and skidded, flames nipping at her limbs. Desperate, St. Cyprian brought his legs up between himself and the monster and shoved it back.

It staggered away from him and he rose, snatching up a chunk of burning wood, ignoring the heat and the smell of his palms burning. Coughing, he drove the monster back as fire rained down around them. Nephren-Ka whined in what might have been either agony or fear and then St. Cyprian drove the burning wood into the creature's damnable eyes, causing it to reel back and howl.

St. Cyprian heard wood crack, and jumped back just in time as a piece of the ceiling came hurtling down like a comet, separating he and Nephren-Ka. He lost sight of the creature as the fire drove him back. It was a dim, flailing smudge, trapped in the heart of the inferno. The Black Pharaoh's howls spiraled up, rising even above the hungry crackle of the flames and then

135

the house gave vent to a moan and a flush of heated air drove him back further from the room. Smoke tore at his lungs and nose. Coughing and partially blinded, he staggered towards the exit, in pursuit of Gallowglass, who had gotten to her feet and scrambled for the door.

He reached the exit and bells rang as the cool, open air greeted him. Someone had called the fire brigade. People ran to and fro in the street and a bucket chain was being formed. "Gallowglass," he coughed as he staggered away from the house. He felt her grab his arm and she led him away from the fire. His hands ached and his throat felt raw, inside and out.

"Here," she said, helping him sit down on the pavement opposite the burning house. Her soot-smudged face broke into a weak grin. "Are all unwrapping parties so much fun?"

"No," St. Cyprian muttered, still coughing.

Her grin faded as she took in the flames. The flames rushed up through the roof and out through the busted windows and door. "What the hell was that thing?" she said.

"Something that should have stayed where it was," he said. "Something even a fool like Bellingham should have known better than to dig up." He wondered where the Grand Vizier of the Esoteric Order of Thoth-Ra had gone. Hopefully back to the Sudan, if Providence were kind.

"Think that thing is dead?" she said, more quietly.

St. Cyprian didn't reply for a moment. He watched the flames crawl from towards nearby buildings and he hoped the whole block would go up in smoke. Even then, there was no way to be sure. He looked down at his cracked and blistered hands. *It was already dead*, he wanted to say. And what was dead could likely eternal lie, to misquote Alhazred.

"I hope so, Miss Gallowglass. I really do."

GABRIEL'S TRUMPET

TRUMPET

Jon Black

Digging Up a Grave...

A Preview of

Jon Black's Gabriel's Trumpet

Marcus had hoped for a lengthier stay at Eden Plantation. With unexpected time on his hands, he asked Bartholomew how far out of their way the Gibbs place was. When the driver indicated not too terribly, Marcus decided to drop in on the family.

Leaving the River Road, Bartholomew confidently negotiated backcountry roads as well as old wagon tracks that were little more than parallel ruts running between fields of cut cotton. Occasionally, they passed through one-store hamlets that appeared stuck in the final decade of the last century. When, at last, the driver put the wagon onto Lula Pike, it was less than a quarter mile from the Gibbs spread. Marcus marveled at the driver's knowledge of the obscure byways and corners of Gates County.

They found the Gibbs household busy with preparations to visit family friends for Saturday supper. In spite of the frantic activity, Sam made time to fill Marcus in on the next chapter in his brother's life.

"Everything came to a head when King Oliver came to town," he explained while polishing his good shoes. "As a gimmick to promote his new recordings, Gennett Records sent King Oliver all over the country judging jazz trumpet contests. The prize was $10. But each local contest winner got to play against the King for $100. Of course, nobody won that prize. Well, almost nobody…

"That morning, Gabe showed up at the county fairgrounds where King Oliver was holding his big to-do. And he wasn't alone. Every trumpet blower in Gates County came. Underbluff was a ghost town that day. Even a few white players turned up. And, I'll tell you, some of them weren't half-bad. But one contestant took everyone's breath away just by being there. Pastor Heulen himself, in the flesh. After everything he'd said about worldly music. All I can figure is that his pride couldn't abide it if Gabriel got named Gates County's best trumpeter. No man knows what he's worth 'til he's tested. And it seemed like his pride proved to mean more to Pastor than anything else.

"From the first, the real contest was between Gabe and Pastor. The way the contest was supposed to work, each contestant would play a piece. When everyone had played, King Oliver would dismiss some of them. Then the ones that remained would play another piece. And so on. Until the King declared somebody the winner.

"But Gabe and Pastor couldn't leave each other alone. Each kept barging in while the other one played. Pretty soon, it turned into a cutting contest between the two of them. Both playing back and forth, playing off each other but trying to outdo each other. Those weren't the rules.

But, seeing how fired up it got the crowd, King Oliver just let it go.

"In a lot of ways, it was just like when the two of them used to duet in the parlor. Except now, instead of trying to build each other up, each was trying to tear the other down. They played like men possessed, like their lives depended on it. In a way, maybe they did," as Sam spoke, he helped Hannah pack two loaves of bread and a peach pie into a wicker basket, covering it with a checkered cloth. "Both of them were magnificent. But Gabe knew jazz better. Maybe he wanted it more, too. When the last note faded, King Oliver declared my brother the winner."

"Squaring off against King Oliver, Gabe did something risky, playing nothing but the King's own tunes. In most ways, he just matched King Oliver. But everyone thrilled at his long, bold notes. It was like my brother was challenging the King to do the same. Well, Gabe held those notes longer and bolder than he could. Red Allen, King Oliver's junior trumpeter, judged the contest. He had to acknowledge his own bandleader was beaten by Gabe.

"As for Pastor Heulen, he'd staked everything and lost. He knew it. His flock knew it too. He tried to keep the tabernacle going. But folks drifted away. And the ones who had been his most fervent supporters were the first to go." Sam halted his tale as he and Henrietta straightened their daughters' dresses and subjected them to a final inspection. "A year gone by, the tabernacle's doors shut for good.

141

Pastor Heulen became a recluse and eventually disappeared. Rumor says he's preaching somewhere else now: Clarksdale, Panther Burn, Tutwiler, even all the way down in Jackson.

"Gabe took that $100 and made his way to New Orleans. 'The bigtime,' as he said." With that, Sam excused himself. Marcus watched him help the children and Aunt Mancie into the old farm truck. Sliding behind the wheel, Pa Gibbs brought the thing to life and sent it rolling down the pike.

Marcus and Bartholomew returned to Pilate's Point with daylight remaining. While he had received useful information both from Colonel Scobie and Sam Gibbs, the day's general turn of events left Marcus frustrated. Hoping to turn his luck around, after reconfirming their arrangement for him to borrow Figaro and the wagon the following morning, Marcus asked the driver to drop him off at the Gates County Sheriff's office.

He wanted to follow up on things learned at the historical society, Eden Plantation, and, most of all, the Episcopal churchyard. The Scobie Mausoleum stood foremost in his thoughts. It didn't appear to have been broken in to or vandalized. But, if it had been, Sheriff Caldwell would know.

It surprised Marcus to find the congenial, if heavily guarded, demeanor the sheriff displayed on their first meeting replaced with storm clouds. "I know you've got a job to do," Sheriff Caldwell began forcefully, "but leave Colonel

Scobie alone. The Scobies are an honorable family and don't deserve rumors circulating because of some outsider poking around. Amicus Scobie has led a good, respectable life. He's an old man now and doesn't need people upsetting him."

Somehow the sheriff knew of his visit to Eden Plantation. Marcus was tempted to argue with him. But the lawman's face suggested his odds weren't good. Based on everything Marcus had heard about Southern tempers, he decided not to press the point.

Despondently, Marcus returned to the Mississippian Hotel. Few things could have further soured his mood at that point. Unfortunately, another exchange with Theodore Fenno was one of them. Entering through the lobby door, the ASPR man carried a variety of cones, bells, and other odd equipment. Marcus also noted the dust and mud coating the New Yorker's boots.

"I thought you said your investigation here was almost complete?" Marcus jibbed. Perhaps it was unseemly, but he enjoyed the sensation of striking the first blow for once.

"Taunt all you want, fishmonger. I've been to the crossroads. I know its secrets," Fenno gloated. "That's the problem with you BSPR people. You're afraid to get your hands dirty."

Laughing at Fenno, Marcus noticed an edge to his laughter that was more manic than mirthful. Hearing the same, his rival instinctively shirked away. As Fenno departed, Marcus wondered how the socially correct

Knickerbocker would react if he knew exactly how dirty Marcus's hands would soon become.

Shortly after sunup, Marcus paid a call on Bartholomew to pick up Figaro and the wagon. It came as a surprise to find the driver wearing pressed-pants and buttoning up a well-starched shirt. "I wouldn't have figured you for a church goer," Marcus teased lightly but honestly. He remembered the comment Sam Gibbs had made during their first meeting. Maybe Marcus really didn't understand about church here.

"Well, it hasn't done me much good, yet," the driver acknowledged, "but I keep hoping." After a pause, he asked "How'd your visit with the sheriff turn out yesterday?"

Marcus recounted his exchange with Sheriff Caldwell, particularly the lawman's firm instructions not to further trouble Colonel Scobie. When Marcus finished the tale, Bartholomew broke into laughter at once childlike in its spontaneity and cynical in its worldliness.

"What's so funny?"

"'Good, respectable life?' Colonel Scobie is the biggest rumrunner in Gates County," the driver replied.

"How do you know that?"

"Everybody knows that. Might be that I know from more experience than most."

Marcus thought that over for a moment. Bartholomew's strange comings and odd deliveries. His familiarity with Gates Country's obscure, thinly-populated areas. And his widely

144

recognized face. All of those suddenly made a great deal more sense. Bartholomew's revelation also shed light on the reversal of Eden Plantation's declining fortunes. Starting about a decade ago, the turnaround coincided neatly with the onset of Prohibition.

"Might even be," the driver added with a wink "that's how I got to know Gabriel."

"Gabriel moved moonshine for the Colonel?"

Bartholomew nodded. "He wanted to earn extra money for that move to New Orleans or New York he always talked about."

To hear Bartholomew tell it now, Scobie's elegant plantation was not so much a showpiece as a front for modern commerce of the illicit kind. A staging area for bringing hooch down from Memphis or up from New Orleans and the Gulf. And distributing it not just in Gates County, but much of northwest Mississippi.

Gibbs' involvement with Colonel Scobie hadn't started out on the sly as far as Bartholomew knew. Initially, the Colonel was interested only in his music, hiring the trumpeter to play at his frequent parties, balls, and soirees.

But the musician was smart and observant. It didn't take him long to discover the Colonel's other activities. When he figured out how much money could be made in running moonshine, he wanted in. Colonel Scobie must have had a good feeling about the young man. The wily old veteran placed a lot of trust in the musician very quickly.

"Is that what was behind his disappearances? And the sightings of him in strange locations and at odd times?" Marcus wanted to know.

"Some of them, anyway. I can't say for certain about every time," he went silent for a moment. "I will tell you this. Gabriel and I were good friends for a time. We used to talk about our dreams. Me about how I would marry my lady friend and become a respectable fellow. Him about moving on to New York or New Orleans. How he was going to be a big shot musician one day. But he was different after he had that trumpet. Quieter. Didn't want to talk as much. Like he had some big secret."

Bartholomew excused himself and made his way to church. Their exchange gave Marcus much to ponder as he climbed up to the buckboard and set the wagon in motion. At first uncomfortable about a stranger guiding him, Figaro soon grew pliant under Marcus's command. No expert driver, Marcus could still manage a wagon along Gates County's sleepy byways. As Pilate's Point faded into the distance, Marcus followed the directions given to him earlier by Sam Gibbs.

The Ascending Glory Tabernacle, what remained of it, was a long, narrow box. A covered porch protected double doors at one end. An obelisk-like steeple jutted heavenward at the other. Faded whitewash peeled from weathered boards. Weeds, brambles, and sickly sunflowers grew on its grounds. Only the churchyard remained well tended.

There was no particular reason Marcus needed to see the tabernacle. The building itself had no specific bearing on his investigation of

146

Gabriel Gibbs. The *story* of Gabriel Gibbs was another matter entirely. This place, and the now vanished clergyman who had ruled over it, were fundamental to understanding the young musician's life. Perhaps he was becoming a romantic as he aged, but Marcus had needed to see the tabernacle. To make it real to him. Even now, he could almost hear singing coming from inside the ruin. A little too well, in fact. Though the morning had already started to swelter, a chilly tingle traveled down Marcus's spine. Taking reins in hand, he turned the wagon away.

Leaving the tabernacle behind, Marcus guided Figaro along the dusty rural path known as Old Terraplane Highway. He came to where a rutted dirt track intersected the main road, itself not much more than packed earth barely wide enough for two wagons to pass abreast.

Though he had passed several such crossroads already, a massive, twisted oak set this one apart. As Marcus approached, other differences appeared. Opposite the tree were low mounds capped with grayed and weathered wooden crosses. Graves, Marcus realized. In archaic traditions, which it seemed had not fully died out here, those considered unworthy of hallowed ground were often interred at crossroads. If Gabriel Gibbs had died before the creation of a county cemetery, he might well have been buried here. Who had been laid to rest under those mounds? What stories would they tell? Marcus mused that he was indeed becoming a romantic.

A strange assortment of objects adorned the

tree, primarily candles and liquor bottles. But a few more puzzling items stood out. A heart-shaped locket dangled from a branch. A knife protruded from the earth at the oak's roots. Nearby, a ragdoll slowly moldered from exposure to the elements.

Cleary, this was *the* crossroad. The one whispered about in relation to Gabriel Gibbs. But what did it all mean? Marcus thought it a pity that Frazer's *Golden Bough* never seriously treated the societies of the New World…and that the curmudgeonly Scottish anthropologist thought of folklore as something inhabiting the increasingly distant country of the past rather than infusing the living world all around him.

Minutes beyond the crossroad, Old Terraplane Highway rejoined the main road. From there, a few more miles took him back to Terraplane, the town where his Gates County adventures had begun.

Driving the wagon into the larger town, a chorus of church bells, both great and humble, flooded his ears. Marcus had intended to do some shopping here, but the ringing bells announced an unanticipated hitch in his plans. Stores in Gates County closed on Sunday. Nevertheless, certain items were essential for his activities. With a little looking around, and light fingers, Marcus "liberated" what he needed: canvas tarp, a crowbar, hooded lantern, pick, and shovel. "All in the name of science," he told himself, hoping no one would suffer too much from his pilfering. Hanging the lantern from the wagon, he loaded the tools in its bed beside

Bartholomew's various deliveries for tomorrow. Not wanting awkward questions, Marcus covered his acquisitions with the tarp.

He traveled eastward to the community of Venice, Gabriel's birthplace. Arriving late in the afternoon, he found nothing more than a sad collection of tarpaper shacks and a company store serving nearby Venice Planation. When nobody there seemed to recall much about the Gibbs family, Marcus was only too happy to turn the wagon around. Darkness descending, he lit the lantern.

Homeward bound, Marcus again passed the crossroad. By night, the gnarled oak assumed a sinister shape. Wind teased the tall grass atop unhallowed graves and caused the oak's branches to reach for him. His skin crawled. The Delta had a power, one Marcus also encountered in remote pockets of New England, rendering the mundane damnably suggestive. Little wonder the region was so steeped in folklore. It didn't make his final task, the real reason for his solo excursion, any more appealing.

His pocket watch showed just after midnight as the wagon stopped beneath a faded wooden sign that proclaimed "Gates County Cemetery, Est. 1898." Or it would have, had negligence or ghoulish vandalism not absconded with several letters, leaving behind only the "Gat s Coun y Cemeter."

Marcus hooded his lantern so it cast only a thin, directional beam.

A wire fence marked off the cemetery grounds. To one side stood a small gate. Directly

149

underneath the cemetery sign was another, wider gate. The "corpse gate," as such features had been known until just a few generations ago, served those who only needed to use it once. Except, perhaps, in the case of Gabriel Gibbs.

After cleaning his glasses several times, Marcus removed the tarp, revealing the crowbar, shovel, and pick in the wagon's bed.

To determine if a man documented as dead had returned to the living, Marcus had resigned himself, it was very useful to know what, if anything, his grave contained. Not allowing himself time to think, he set about the repellent task.

As he carried his tools from the wagon, noises behind Marcus brought him to a halt. Horrified, he watched a figure emerge from the bushes. Of all the people he might have expected to encounter here, Aunt Mancie was not on the list. In the lamplight, the Gibbs family matriarch appeared far more vigorous and hearty than on her rocking chair.

"Aunt Mancie, what are you doing here?"

"How come you never asked me about Gabriel?" she challenged him. "You figure the crazy old woman doesn't know anything?"

He hadn't realized it at the time, but her words held much truth. Marcus had the decency to look embarrassed.

"Doesn't matter now," she said. "I reckoned sooner or later you'd turn up here."

"Why?"

"If I wanted to see if someone was alive or dead, I'd look here," she said plainly. "And, if

150

you're opening my grandnephew's grave, it seems only proper that a family member bears witness."

"You didn't tell the others?"

"They might have stopped you."

"You're not going to?"

"Truth is, I'm curious, too."

Digging up a grave was among the hardest, dirtiest things Marcus had done. Taking a break to catch his breath, Marcus looked at his unexpected companion. "Aunt Mancie, do you believe it's possible for people to come back from the dead?"

"Almost anything you can say is possible. Whether it's likely is another thing entirely. And, please, when we're not on the porch you can forget about the 'Aunt' Mancie nonsense."

Hours later, he bent over the exposed coffin of Gabriel Gibbs, holding his crowbar. Standing over the hole, Mancie cradled the pick as if on guard duty. Guarding against what? Marcus didn't ask. He was pretty sure he didn't want to know.

Holding his breath, he wedged the crowbar underneath the coffin lid and pushed down. The lid swung open smoothly, offering no resistance, as if it had been forced before. Discovering it to be empty, Mancie and Marcus exhaled in unison, whether out of surprise, relief, or a mixture of both.

Not only was the coffin unoccupied, its upholstered interior remained unsoiled. As a physician, Marcus was familiar with death and what accompanied it. A body had not lain here, or not lain long enough for decay to leave its mark.

"Mancie, would you pass me the lantern?"

Taking the light from the matriarch, Marcus illuminated the coffin's interior. His careful examination revealed dark hairs and a small fingernail ripped from its owner during some epic endeavor. Breaking out? Breaking in? That was the question. But someone had been here. If not Gibbs himself, then whom? And to what purpose? Marcus pocketed the samples, hoping his companion would not notice.

"Can I offer you a ride?" he asked Mancie after covering up the evidence of their deed.

"I hoped you were that much of a gentleman," she replied.

Marcus enjoyed the trip immensely. The old woman, who had stopped seeming so old hours earlier, owned a lively intellect and great curiosity. She questioned Marcus about Boston and his career as a physician. She inquired into his work with the BSPR, appreciating his answers better than most people. In return, she regaled him with local folklore of a distinctly esoteric nature: giant snakes, Hill Folk, Ol' Bloody Bones, Rougaroux, the Singing River, Skunk Apes, Two-Toed Tom, and variations of the ubiquitous ghosts, vampires, and witches.

"Do you believe in any of those things?" he asked.

"It's like I told you back in the burying yard," she replied. "Anything is possible. What's actual is a different matter entirely." She kept her peace for a moment. "But I have a few opinions that might surprise you."

Marcus was uncertain if she teased him. When she refused to be drawn out any further on the matter, he switched topics. "I've never encountered the name Mancie before. What does it mean? Is it short for something?"

"My momma, God rest her soul, went into labor while the Federals swept across Gates County. Right as Union troops were fighting to take Venice Plantation from Nathan Forrest's bushwhackers, in fact. Gunfire going off all around her shack, she held me in her body until the fighting ended and the Blues had taken the place. She swore her baby girl, and somehow she knew I'd be a girl, would be born a free woman. She named me 'Emancipation.' That's quite a mouthful for a child. All I could manage was 'Mancie,' so that's what it's been ever since."

As conversation drifted back toward her grandnephew, Mancie supplied the remaining Gates County parts of the tale. "When Gabriel reached New Orleans, he wrote us that he was playing at someplace called L'Original," she recounted. "He didn't say so, but we knew it was just some Storyville bawdyhouse. Not much came after that. One day, we got the telegram saying he died. Was murdered. Rebekah went to down to bring him home.

"When she got back, an awful fuss occurred. Pastor Heulen had gone and the tabernacle shut, but a lot of people didn't want Gabriel in the churchyard. They still told those stories about him. We had to bury him in that county cemetery back there.

"Poor Rebekah was never right again. Just slipped into her own world. She chatted with Gabriel like he was there beside her. And, like her brother had, she took to wandering. Soon after, she just disappeared. We got a letter from the State Hospital telling us Rebekah had been found, completely senseless, over in Panola County and been committed. Every so often we get a letter from her. Every so often we write. But she's not what you'd call lucid.

"A year gone by, we started hearing rumors. Someone spotted Gabriel in New Orleans. Or Jackson. Then New York. Gabriel, or whoever, was playing that silver trumpet and telling folks he'd 'come back.' We didn't know what to make of it. None of us have seen him. But a lot of folks have their notions and know exactly what they make of it."

Interrupting Mancie's tale, three sets of headlights blinded Figaro and his passengers. Through the glare, Marcus could make out a trio of Model T automobiles and maybe a dozen men. There were words for a group like this: a mob.

"Look a damn Yankee," one shouted, pronouncing the last two words as one, before offering less savoy comments about Mancie. "Two birds with one stone," another man said as the mob closed in on their wagon.

Mancie looked at Marcus. "How good are you at driving a wagon?" she asked. When he hesitated, Mancie grabbed the reins, swinging the wagon around in a single, fluid motion. With a stern "Get!" she sent Figaro pulling them down the road at backbreaking speed.

Rushing to their automobiles, the men gave chase.

"Climb into the bed and see if anything back there will do us any good," Mancie shouted.

Doing so, he examined Bartholomew's goods. In addition to the tools Marcus had liberated in Terraplane, some of which would make serviceable weapons if the worst happened, he found loose lumber and two barrels. One contained clout nails, likely part of the same load as the lumber. Flour filled the second barrel. Marcus grinned. He could work with these.

Groaning, he tilted the second barrel against the backboard, tipping out 300 pounds of flour. A cloud of flour dust now hanging over the road, Marcus could no longer see his pursuers. Presumably, the reverse was also true. He then dumped the other barrel as well. He noted with satisfaction that about a fourth of the short-shafted, broad-headed nails landed point upward.

The cars roared out from the dust cloud and over the nails. Staccato sequences of hollow pops proclaimed the death of tires. The first automobile came to a hard stop in a ditch. The second spun out of control, rolling over on its side as men scrambled from the wreck. Witnessing the fate of its fellows, the third Model T swerved into the fields, avoiding the hazard, before returning to the road.

Fortunately, Gates County's rutted dirt roads were as hard on cars as horses. Driving Figaro as fiercely as she could, Mancie maintained their lead over the Model T. Unfortunately, animals tired. Automobiles didn't.

As the road passed through woods, Mancie shouted to Marcus "Follow my lead!" Standing on the buckboard, reins in one hand, she hiked up her skirt with the other. With a wild yell, she leapt onto Figaro's back.

Moving to the buckboard, Marcus hesitated. The five-foot jump looked impossibly distant. "Dr. Roads, let me suggest that this is an excellent time to grow a pair," Mancie yelled. Marcus jumped. Landing hard on the animal's back, Marcus concluded no, it was distinctly not a good a time to grow a pair.

Unhitching Figaro from the wagon, Mancie grabbed Marcus's arm and put it around her waist. She guided the horse off into the trees. Behind them, Marcus heard the Model T screech to a halt, its occupants cursing.

Mancie led Figaro through woods and fields on an oblique route to town. Once safely in Underbluff, Marcus checked his pocket watch. Its hands informed him that dawn neared. His body screamed that was a lie, the night had been the longest week of Marcus Roads' life.

As he tied-up Figaro outside of Bartholomew's place, Marcus didn't look forward to the conversation he'd have with the driver tomorrow. He observed Mancie studying him. "Everything fine?" he asked.

156

He couldn't quite make out her reply, spoken to herself more than Marcus. He thought she said, "Just wondering if you're old enough for me."

After escorting Mancie to Midtown, where she'd spend the night with a family friend, Marcus dragged himself back to the Mississippian Hotel.

Waking at mid-morning, Marcus immediately checked on Mancie. Sore but otherwise unharmed, the pair strolled and discussed the previous evening's events. As they walked, Marcus struggled to find the right words for asking another question about Gabriel. He prefaced it by recalling what Sam Gibbs had said about the difference between church music and worldly music. As he grappled with expressing those still unfamiliar concepts in his own terms, Mancie gave him a look that while, gracious, clearly meant "I know all that. Get to your point."

"When Gabriel made his decision. When he renounced Pastor Huelen to play jazz," Marcus began, "was he really rejecting God and the church as well? Or did he not see it like that?"

"That is a good question," Mancie acknowledged, falling silent as she thought it over. "No person ever really knows another person's soul. And my grand-nephew's soul was harder to know than most. But I don't believe, when Gabriel stood in the tabernacle that final time, he thought he was choosing the world over the church. Old Jericho Heulen would have

157

hated that but at least he could have understood it. What enraged the pastor, maybe even frightened him, was the notion that Gabriel saw music as something 'other.' Something existing outside of sin and salvation. And that maybe music was more important to Gabriel than either of those."

A familiar face derailed their conversation. It was the man's limp that first drew Marcus's attention. A limp acquired, no doubt, when his Model T overturned the night before. In fact, if Marcus was correct, this man had made the "Two birds, one stone" crack.

The man didn't notice him until Marcus put a hand on his shoulder and spun him around. As his injured leg gave out, the man tumbled to the ground. Deducing the leg must be bad indeed, Marcus had an idea. "I don't believe we've been properly introduced." Marcus grinned as he put his full weight on the limb. "We met last night."

Wincing with pain, the man nodded.

"You know I'm a doctor?"

He shook his head.

"The way you're reacting, I suspect that leg is fractured badly. There's a good chance you'll lose it unless you have a doctor set it. Do you have money for a doctor?"

Again, the man shook his head.

"I'll set that bone for you, if you tell me about last night. Do we have an understanding?"

He nodded warily.

Marcus rigged a splint from handy materials and the contents of his black bag. As Marcus worked, the man spilled his guts. He and his companions had been paid five dollars each to scare Marcus, maybe rough him up a bit, but not do any lasting harm. "We didn't expect you to be with anybody else. Or go and pull all those crazy stunts," the man said as if it excused his behavior and he was the aggrieved the party. It didn't and he wasn't.

"Who paid you?" Marcus demanded. His mind ran through the list of possible suspects. The sheriff was unhappy with him. The hotel manager, too. But neither seemed upset enough to try something like this. Or had the supposedly-ill Colonel Scobie feared Marcus might learn too much about his bootlegging operation?

"Some other damn Yankee." Again, the last two words pronounced as one.

"Oh," Marcus replied, his voice venomous. The man had held up his end of the bargain. Marcus turned him loose, saying "You're good to go. Try not to lift anything heavy for two weeks and no running for a month." After pausing, he added, "And I would suggest not making any more trouble for me or for this nice lady. Remember, we both know exactly where to hit your leg to break it again."

"Yes, sir," he groveled resentfully before hobbling away as rapidly as his splint allowed.

"That took ice-cold nerve, threatening a man with losing his leg," Mancie said approvingly.

"It would, if it was true," Marcus answered. "That's not how you treat a fracture. Not even close. He has nothing but a bad sprain. Not that he needed to know that."

159

Mancie laughed. "Marcus Roads, I believe you may do alright out in the world."